MISS ETTA'S

For Reference

Not to be taken from this room

GEORGE IMBRAGULIO

Miss Etta's Arkansas Spring

FITHIAN PRESS
SANTA BARBARA • 1999

COPYRIGHT ©1999 by George Imbragulio
ALL RIGHTS RESERVED
PRINTED IN THE UNITED STATES OF AMERICA

DESIGN AND TYPOGRAPHY BY JIM COOK

Published by Fithian Press
A division of Daniel & Daniel, Publishers, Inc.
Post Office Box 1525
Santa Barbara, California 93102

LIBRARY OF CONGRESS CATALOGING-IN-PUBLICATION DATA
Imbragulio, George, (date)
Miss Etta's Arkansas spring :
a novel / by George Imbragulio.
p. cm.
ISBN 1-56474-283-0 (ALK. PAPER)
I. TITLE.
PS3559.M47M5 1999
813'.54—DC 21
98-27398
CIP

Dedicated to those who inspired it,
the members of the
National Guild of Piano Teachers . . .
especially the lonely ones.

Prologue

THE CONTINUOUS LIGHTNING AND THUNDER had already shocked her awake. She reached over to pick up her Raggedy Ann doll and squeezed it as hard as she could against her body and listened with growing fear to the whining of the wind. The window panes rattled and the dry chinaberry limbs scratched sandpaper sounds against the sides of the house like somebody trying to get in. If she had but blinked her eyes, she wouldn't have seen it. A filament of lightning pierced the cold darkness with a brittle snap like the cracking of a whip and singled out some object near the dresser. Screaming, she jumped from the bed and elbowed her way under it, holding the doll by one of its limp arms.

Fast footsteps, like amplified, erratic heartbeats, came down the hall. Her mother threw open the door. "Fayetta Rose! Get up right this minute and get dressed! The 'lectricity's off and a storm's comin' and you gotta hurry! . . . Fayetta, where are you?"

"Under the bed, Mamma. I'm scared."

"Well, get yourself out from under there right this minute and hurry. You've got to hurry or we'll all be killed. Hurry!"

She crawled from beneath the bed, dragging her doll with her, crying and all of a sudden feeling all alone. As she fumbled with her dress, another bolt of lightning split the air and a sharp, high-pitched explosion of thunder battered her eardrums and echoed through the house. She was too scared to button herself up. She must run as fast as she could.

She stopped to pick up her doll and heard what sounded like a train coming at full speed down the street in front of the house. She held on to the bed and started to feel her way out of the room when some monstrous force with the strength and sound of not one but a hundred locomotives hit the house broadside. She fell to the floor, crouched forward with her head between her knees and her arms bent back over her head. When she finally moved and opened her eyes, she realized the roof of the house had been ripped off and the rain was pouring in cold torrents all over her. She screamed at the top of her lungs, "Mamma! Mamma! Help me!" Suddenly, she lost consciousness.

When she came to, she tried to stand, reaching out for the bedpost. It was not there. She strained to see. It must be a bad dream, she thought, and tried hard to remember. She pulled herself up and tried to find her way out the bedroom door. It was jammed. She pulled with all her strength, screaming, feeling the cold wetness of her soaked clothing. She pushed through the small space between the door and the facing, felt her dress tear as she slithered through, and ran toward her parents' bedroom. She fell time and time again. The floor was bucked up and pieces of furniture and broken power lines were scattered everywhere.

Just as she neared the bedroom, still screaming and calling them to help her, she fell forward over a huge object. There was no sound from inside the room. The storm had passed and now everything was deathly still and quiet. She pushed and pulled on the heavy object blocking the bedroom door but to no avail. She covered her face with both hands and collapsed to the floor.

The tornado had devastated the little town of Gloster, Arkansas. Fayetta Rose did not know until three days later that the heavy object blocking the door of her parents' room was the attic fan and that behind the door, clinging to each other under a ton of wreckage, were her father and mother.

After the funeral and after what remained of the family belongings was collected and sold or given to the Salvation Army, Fayetta Rose's aunt Clara took her to Blytheville to live with her and her four children. Little Fayetta Rose Ramsey was seven years old at the time. She lived through the transition and for the following seven months in a state of emotional numbness, during which time she never spoke a word.

Miss Etta's Arkansas Spring

1

THE WIDOW ARMSTRONG, AFFECTIONATELY known to her friends and students as Miss Etta, put the finishing touches to her uniformly white and slightly wavy hair, drank the last of her breakfast coffee, and wiped the corners of her mouth with a starchy white napkin. She stood before the full-length mirror affixed to the door leading from her bedroom to the bath and gave a nip and a tuck here and there and one more thoughtless touch to her hair. She half listened to the morning news on her bedside radio. She was more interested in the weather report that would follow. The annual Guild auditions were scheduled for next week and, as chairperson of the local chapter, she wanted the weather, like everything else, to be perfect.

It was almost seven o'clock and time for little Mary Beth Simmons, her first student of the day. Mary Beth had to take her lesson before school because of other commitments she or her mother had after school. She was one of three students coming this morning.

The weather news wasn't encouraging. A developing storm system over the Texas panhandle would shortly be moving eastward with the likely possibility that some hazardous weather would be making its way into the state late Sunday evening or Monday morning. The threat of bad weather always distressed her. It seemed the weather had become much more severe over the past few years and the frequency of tornadoes greatly increased. Her concern had increased proportionately. After all, she thought as she picked up the empty cup and the napkin and started to the kitchen, this is the tornado season. She made a quick resolve not to become too concerned. Weather forecasts, after all, were often wrong.

She quickly returned to her bedroom upon remembering she had not applied her usual drop of cologne, that unidentifiable, nondescript fragrance with which she had been associated for as long as she had lived in Montcrief, Arkansas. People who talked about her almost always made some reference to her perfume. It was not pungent but seemed to combine the subtle scents of sweet peas, lavender, and something slightly medicinal.

As she turned to leave the bedroom, she saw the letter from her daughter Annette which came yesterday, and walked over and picked it up. She was suddenly overcome by a dark feeling that had intensified each time she read it. She started to take it from the envelope again but, instead, laid it on the letter rack on the desk and looked pensively out the window.

It had come at such a bad time, just when she needed to give all of her attention and energy to the auditions, like a dark cloud suddenly appearing for no good reason in a perfectly clear, bright sky. She pondered the contents of the letter and considered the consequences, letting her imagination spring out in every direction to conceive the most horrible possibilities. Yet, as she stood there, letting the letter upset her more and more, she was aware that the source of her distress was not simply what Annette had said. Each letter from Annette, even the happiest ones, was laced with a dark edge of discontent. She must never verbalize that ugly thing, yet it lay always at the back of her mind like a low-grade pain that never goes away.

The doorbell rang just as she was adjusting her glasses and coiffing her hair precisely over her ears. It rang not once, but several times, continuously. Her slight ninety-two pounds hardly caused a sound as she hurried to open the front door.

"Good mornin', Mary Beth," she half sang, holding the screen door with one hand and affectionately laying the other on Mary

Beth's abundant red hair. "My goodness, that's a mighty pretty dress you've got on." She latched the screen door. "I bet it's new, isn't it? Did mother make it for you?"

Not a word from Mary Beth. Just a mean look and two or three quick nods of her little red head. She never talked very much, even less first thing of a morning. Behind the surly countenance was an uncommonly strong aversion to Miss Etta Armstrong and what she stood for. Taking piano lessons had not been her idea in the first place but her mother's. Lucille Simmons had studied piano with Miss Etta years ago. In a little town where cultural opportunities were all but non-existent, taking piano lessons was considered essential for young ladies. There was always some question about why little boys did it.

Mary Beth sat down at the old sun-seared grand piano and, without waiting to be told what to do, started playing the only one of her three pieces she liked. It was an immensely popular piece called "Jukebox Jamboree" that was currently making the rounds. She had liked it the moment she first heard it. She thought the jazzy rhythm was neat and could hardly wait to learn it so she could impress her friends. There were a few. It was useless for Miss Etta to try to tell her all the things she was doing wrong. She had created her own version, and Mary Beth didn't take suggestions too well anyway.

"Now, now, Mary Beth," Miss Etta admonished playfully. "Aren't we forgettin' somethin'?" She pulled her chair up closer to Mary Beth's side.

Mary Beth had either not heard, didn't care, or both. She kept right on going with her paraphrase of "Jukebox Jamboree." Miss Etta reached up and pulled the piece from the music rack, closed it deliberately, and pressed it to her flat bosom. Mary Beth came down with both hands on the keys and kicked the pedal board with her feet.

"Now, now, Mary Beth, let's not be a naughty little girl." She gently laid a hand on the little girl's shoulder. Mary Beth quickly shrugged and knocked it off. You just didn't do things like that to Mary Beth. Especially not this early in the day.

Miss Etta remained sweetly firm. "You know nice little girls don't throw tantrums. . . . Now." She replaced the music on the rack. "I was only tryin' to remind you that we don't just come in, sit down, and start playin' at our lessons. And furthermore, you know the Guild requires us to play our scales first."

Mary Beth stomped the floor with her dirty little sneakers. "I don't care what the old Guild says," she screamed. Then a half-octave higher, "I don't care! I don't care! I hate them old scales and I ain't gonna play 'em. So there!" With which she kicked the pedal board again.

Miss Etta sighed deeply and looked out the window. The purple irises were blooming this side of the garage and the peach tree just outside the window was full of radiant pink blossoms. She wished somehow that she were one of those peach blossoms. Or that little wren sitting serenely still on the telephone wire. She smiled without realizing she was doing so. Long ago she had learned that smiling often has an antidotal effect on her spirit.

"All right, Mary Beth. Miss Etta won't say anymore." She reached over and removed a torn scrap of Mary Beth's music from the keys. "But will you promise Miss Etta that you'll practice the three scales you're supposed to know for your audition? . . . You do remember, don't you, what the Guild judge said last year about you not knowin' your scales? Remember? . . . He said you'd have made a higher score if you'd known them. Remember, dear?"

She assented with a slow nod of her head. She sniffed a time or two, ran a deterrent finger under her runny nose, and resumed her attack on "Jukebox Jamboree."

Before Mary Beth's lesson was over, little Tommy Thornhill, age seven, rang the doorbell. He was always early.

"That'll be Tommy," Miss Etta said to the four walls. "Comin'," she sang as she went to let him in.

"Good mornin', Tommy. How are you, dear?"

"Fine," he said eagerly.

"I'll be right with you, Tommy. In the meantime you just go on in the kitchen and make yourself at home. Get yourself some Coke and cookies. You know where everything is."

Indeed, Tommy knew where everything was. He loved coming to Miss Etta's. He loved all the attention she gave him and the good things she always had to eat and drink. He found playing the piano was a profitable enterprise, a fascinating way to get attention as well as all the things he craved from his parents.

A few minutes later, when Miss Etta had instructed him for the hundredth time about how to sit at the piano and how to pretend he was holding a ball in his little hands and how not to move his hands up and down and how to lift his ten little fingers like ten little soldiers high-stepping on a drill field and how to put a heavy accent on the first beat of every measure and how to let go of a staccato note as though he had touched a hot stove, she assured him he was doing just fine and had much musical talent and promise. She guided him painstakingly and patiently through the two pages of his new method book that had been so highly recommended at the teachers' convention last fall in Little Rock by the man who wrote it. Every detail was pointed out and sweetly stressed upon his bright little brain, even though his bright little brain had lost all interest in piano playing some time ago.

She had waved Tommy goodbye as he got into his mother's car to be taken to school and was now waiting on the porch for her next student, examining some of her many pot plants crowded onto tables and stands here and there. Her next student was Jonell Sumrall.

Jonell was a high school senior with certain privileges the lower grade students didn't enjoy. Like being excused from first period assembly so she could take her piano lesson. The fact that her father was the richest man in Montcrief and politically influential accounted in part for some of the privileges she enjoyed. It was fairly common knowledge that Jonell, the oldest of the three Sumrall children, had proved at an astonishingly early age that she was not capable of handling all the privileges she'd been allowed and had indulged in some hush-hush relationships with many of the not-so-privileged boys in Montcrief. And elsewhere, it was rumored! At one point, in fact, her disappearance from Montcrief for several months had stimulated a great deal of wonder and speculation. When the wonder and speculation had intensified to such a point that her father was annoyed by it, he was rumored to have made a number of serious threats against some of the Montcrief citizenry.

"Mornin', Etta." It was her neighbor Mabel Paradine, not long out of bed, taking her garbage to the curb. After putting the plastic garbage can down, she came over and onto the porch. "Looks like Miss Priss is late again."

Miss Etta smiled and motioned her to one of the rockers. "Well, you know she has that new car her daddy gave her for graduation."

"Yeah, and who don't? But what's that got to do with the price of eggs? Etta, you're so gullible. When are you gonna come to and realize that girl ain't nothin' but a trollop? Why don't you get rid of her?"

Miss Etta winced at the word "trollop" and made a faint, nervous sound in her throat as she eased her small body down into the big, white rocker. "I know. I admit she's not a serious student, but Mabel, she does have some musical talent."

"For God's sake, Etta, so what? That ain't the only kind of talent she's got and you and everybody in Montcrief and Jasper County knows it only too well."

She smiled and turned her face. "I need the money," she said finally with some difficulty.

Unlike Etta, Mable was well-fixed financially. Ernest Paradine had been a shrewd and successful businessman and had made sure before he died that Mabel would be well taken care of. She rocked slowly, looking down at her dew-wet slippers as they rose and fell on the peeling porch floor.

"Heard from Annette lately?"

Annette was married to a university physics professor, had two daughters, and was living in Knoxville, Tennessee. As Mabel soon learned, Annette was a sore topic of conversation.

Miss Etta cleared her throat and slowly, meticulously traced the seams of her plain blue skirt with her slightly gnarled piano-playing fingers. She seemed to be looking at something just beyond the range of her vision. "Well yes, as a matter of fact," she replied. "I got a letter from Annette day before yesterday." She seemed momentarily to lose control of the tiny muscles at the corners of her mouth. She gripped the arms of the rocker.

"Is anything wrong, Etta? She ain't sick, is she? Or the kids? Or Bob?"

"No, not that," she managed hoarsely. "But somethin' she told me has had me upset ever since." Out of her blouse pocket she pulled the neat, lacy handkerchief she carried there. As though determined not to give way completely, she pressed the handkerchief tightly in both hands. "She said she and Bob are goin' to Germany next fall. Bob has a Fulbright teachin' fellowship."

"Oh, Etta!" Mabel reached over and rubbed her hands consolingly. "Oh, what a shame! . . . I mean . . . well, I'm so sorry, honey. No wonder you been upset." She continued looking at Miss Etta's face.

This brought on a little spasm of tears. She carefully removed her glasses and wiped her eyes. She had a delicate nose-blow. "I'm sorry, Mabel. I didn't mean to let my emotions get the better of me." She sat erect with her chin lifted in a way that denoted she was now in control. She wadded the little moist handkerchief into a ball and pressed it against the arm of the chair. This seemed to strengthen her composure. She sniffed a time or two. "You realize gettin' a Fulbright is quite an honor. Bob is such a smart man, and I'm so proud of him." Somewhere deep inside she felt a quick finger-pinch of guilt.

"Of course he is and sure you are," Mabel agreed. "But that means that . . . well, I mean . . . well, you know what I mean, Etta."

She nodded her head and managed a feeble smile as she put her glasses back on and straightened the hair around her ears.

Mabel jumped to her feet as soon as she saw Jonell Sumrall drive up in her new, fire-engine-red Stingray. "I gotta go," she said and made for the steps and sidewalk.

"Mornin', Miz Paradine," Jonell said with a bright smile as they passed each other.

"Mawnin'."

"Good mornin', Miss Etta!" She stretched out the "good." "An' how are you this fantastic spring day?" She took the steps two at a time. She put her free arm around Miss Etta's shoulder as they started into the house. "Say, how you like my new car? Ain't it adorable?"

Miss Etta turned slightly to look at it. "Yes, dear, it surely is. But isn't that one of those fast automobiles? . . . I do hope you'll be careful drivin' it."

"Oh, I will, Miss Etta. You better believe it. That baby cost my daddy a pile of money and I sure aim to take good care of it."

The phone was ringing as they entered.

"Oh, excuse me, Jonell. Let me get that. You go on and start, dear. I'll be there directly."

Jonell preferred to look around. No matter how long she'd been coming for lessons, she was still fascinated by some of the things she saw, smelled, and felt. The ceilings of the old house were extremely high and the walls were papered in faded patterns of scroll work and floral designs. The floors in the living room and dining room were stained dark oak and covered with large area rugs also of floral design and noticeably worn in front of the couch and the heavy velour chairs. The worn spot under the piano pedals had been hidden by an incongruous rubber mat that was hard to keep in place.

The long, narrow windows in the living room were hung with sheer panels and were never opened because the humid Arkansas air was bad for the piano. The brick fireplace, which was no longer used, was painted white and had a black metal panel of ornate design covering the opening. Slight streaks of smoke had stained the bricks surrounding the opening. Above the mantel hung an oak-framed painting of a schooner foundering in a storm, its crew perishing in the raging sea or hanging desperately to the sides of the boat.

She especially liked to look at the assortment of photographs occupying most of the available space on the rough, cracked mahogany tables throughout the room. Some of the pictures were of people she knew or had heard about—Miss Etta's dead husband, her daughter, son-in-law, and two grandchildren, many taken at different stages of their lives. Others were of countless relatives and friends, most of whom had died many years ago and whose obscure likenesses and dress represented a far distant time which mystified and at the same time repulsed her.

For as long as she could remember there had been a distinct odor or combination of odors in this room—from the old, overworked grand piano a suggestion of not-quite-ripe bananas, and from the Duncan Phyfe couch, now covered with a pale green afghan, and the three heavy velour chairs a faintly musty odor. And if you stood in a certain spot, you could often sense from some uncertain source the sharp, wintery smell of mothballs.

Jonell and other students over the years had given Miss Etta a variety of pictures, plaques, or vases bearing music motifs, made in the shape of a musical symbol, or containing inspirational words about music and life. They occupied nearly every available space on the walls, especially that space nearest the piano.

Jonell had just sat down at the piano and was trying to negotiate a popular tune when Miss Etta returned, smiling and radiant.

"That was Mr. Riddick, our Guild judge. He was callin' to find out more about the auditions and wanted to make sure I had him a room at the motel." She hesitated, smiling, and turned to look again at the peach blossoms framed by the long window to her right. "He sounds like such a nice man," she said. And with added enthusiasm, "And he's very handsome as well!"

This disclosure seemed to have a satisfying effect on Jonell. "He is?" she asked, turning so she could look directly into Miss Etta's transformed face. "D'you know him, Miss Etta? . . . You got a picture of him?"

She happily slapped her knees. "Well, sir, as a matter of fact I do. You just wait a minute." She hurried from the room and soon returned with a folder of papers from which she pulled a small, glossy print of Mr. Riddick. She held it as though it were a prized piece of china. "See?" She gave it to Jonell. "He sent two pictures, two different poses. The other one's comin' out tomorrow in the *Herald* along with the article about our auditions."

Jonell was obviously impressed. "Say, he *is* good-lookin'! Just look at that gorgeous hair!" Then with some concern, "But he looks awfully serious to me, don't he to you? How old d'you reckon he is. D'you know?"

Miss Etta took the picture from Jonell and laid it carefully on top of the papers and closed the folder. "Well, no, I don't. I'd say right off-hand he must be around forty. He has a very impressive background. He's studied at some of the finest schools and even spent some time studyin' abroad."

Jonell seemed more than a little interested. For some time her preferences had switched from boys her own age to older, mature men.

When Miss Etta asked her what she had been working on and what she'd like to play, she admitted she really hadn't practiced at all since her last lesson. She'd been having final exams in two or three of her courses and she'd been sick two days and had to stay in bed. One day, just as she started to practice, her mother made her go to the grocery store.

But no matter what folks thought and said about Jonell Sumrall, she had a way of endearing herself to Miss Etta. She gave a husky cigarette laugh and squeezed Miss Etta's hand. "I know you're put out with me, Miss Etta, and I don't blame you one little bit. But I promise you as sure as God made little green apples I'm gonna practice real hard this week and play a good audition and make you proud of me. You just wait and see."

Miss Etta smiled wanly and played distractedly with her hair. She couldn't help feeling guilty when she excused her students from lessons they had already paid for. As compensation, she usually tried to impart some bit of useful information or even some moral guidance, but today, for some unknown reason, she seemed to be resourceless. She pondered a moment, then reached over and gently touched Jonell's arm. "And how's your mother, Jonell?"

Jonell said her mother was doing pretty well, even though she did still complain about her back. "You knew she fell a while back, didn't you?"

Yes, she had heard. It had been rumored that Mr. Sumrall had actually shoved his wife down the stairs during an argument, but Miss Etta chose not to believe it.

"I baked a batch of your favorite cookies last night. You know, the peanut butter ones. Wouldn't you like a few with some Coke before you go to school?" She started to the kitchen. "I bet you haven't had a bite to eat this mornin'."

Jonell declined graciously. She never ate breakfast. She gathered up her music, put an arm around Miss Etta's neck, and gave her a quick kiss on the cheek. "That's awfully sweet of you, but I really must be gettin' on over to school." She'd just have time to smoke a cigarette if she didn't drive too fast.

Miss Etta tried to get her to change her mind but to no avail. Jonell waved goodbye and hurried away, leaving tire marks on the blacktop.

Miss Etta watched absentmindedly for a moment or two, then remembered that Sophronia, her cleaning woman, would be coming soon and she wanted to try to write Annette in the meantime.

2

HER STATIONERY WAS A GIFT FROM ONE of her students, with an unidentifiable fragment of music at the top and various musical symbols lining the left margin. There was little room left for writing. The longer she sat with pen in hand, the more reluctant she was to begin. Her spirit was in a mild state of upheaval. She wrote the date and "Dearest Annette." None of the thoughts running through her head seemed appropriate. She leaned forward, chin on hand, and looked out the window.

The yard looked so beautiful with the graceful curved arms of the chinaberry tree just outside the window contrasting its dark green against the lighter green of the grass and the luxuriant irises in yellow, white, and purple, all in a row separating her yard from Mabel's.

Yet the exhilaration she normally felt each April was being kept in bounds, she realized, and she sensed beyond the next week of auditions and after the spring recital an unsettling emptiness. It was the letter, dropped at her feet unexpectedly, unwanted, and it would stay there, tripping her up every time she tried to be happy, unless she did something about it. But what could she do? If she wrote a reply now, feeling as she did, she would surely betray her grave disappointment and perhaps say something she might later regret.

More importantly still, she might reveal in some unintended way some of the well-guarded and long-suppressed feelings about Bob. She must never do that!

She had resolved many years ago, while living with Aunt Clara and her cousins, to keep her miseries to herself. She had learned very early that other people do not want to know someone else's misery. As the shock and numbness of losing her parents had begun to wear off, she realized there had to be a way to survive in her new environment, even though she didn't like Aunt Clara and her cousins very much. In later years, she found that her early discipline was a real blessing. Now she could accept most adversity with an unmeasurable mote of optimism, though not painlessly. She rarely asked God to change her lot, only that He give her the strength to bear up under it. This is not to say she never wept. She did. Often. But very few people ever saw her do it or knew about it.

When ten-year-old Fayetta Rose first sat down at the tall, mahogany Cable-Nelson piano in Aunt Clara's sunny parlor and began putting together phrases of "The Old Oaken Bucket," the effect was both startling and disturbing. Where on earth the frail, mousey child had come by this talent no one could figure out. Aunt Clara was kind enough to acknowledge the girl's ability yet prudent enough not to allow it to intimidate her own children. Or so she thought.

In time, when some of Aunt Clara's friends convinced her that Fayetta should be given piano lessons and the privilege was provided, two of the other children insisted they also be allowed to take lessons. Fayetta never let it be known, but some of her happiest moments came from hearing her cousins struggling to play their pieces.

Fayetta was soon playing at church and performing more pieces than any of the other students on Mrs. Vandorfer's yearly recitals. The amazing thing was that her talents also included the ability to play by ear. This ultimately stood her in good stead with her cousins, who couldn't conceal the great enjoyment they got from listening to her play the popular tunes of the day and from singing along with her when they felt sufficiently friendly and also knew the words.

One Sunday while her uncle Lester was visiting from Chicago, and after church had been attended and a festive Sunday dinner put away, Aunt Clara asked Fayetta Rose to play for her uncle. Ordinarily Fayetta enjoyed playing for folks, but now she was disinclined. She had seen her uncle only once or twice before, and there was an aura of the big city about him which somehow frightened her. As she was soon to learn, this fear was unfounded.

Uncle Lester knew a lot about human nature and seemed to have decided right away that this seemingly colorless young girl had a beautiful, sensitive nature and a promising musical talent. His opinion, so far, had been based on what he had heard her play at church that morning and his observations of her during his visit. He could see that Clara was going about it the wrong way and adroitly changed the subject. Then, when he felt the time was right, he startled Fayetta and everybody else by asking rather casually, "How would you like me to send you to the Cincinnati Conservatory of Music, Fayetta Rose?"

During her third year at the conservatory, ten days before Thanksgiving, Uncle Lester had a massive heart attack and died. He had neglected to make a will. His holdings were frozen, and Fayetta was compelled to return to her adoptive home. In some ways Uncle Lester's death had been more difficult than that of her parents. His belief in her and his great generosity had touched her profoundly, and she would never fully recover from losing him.

In those days a piano teacher's worth was not determined by the number of college degrees she had earned. As a matter of fact, many of the greatest pianists had no degrees at all. Perhaps certificates or artist diplomas. So, when Fayetta Rose Ramsey returned to Blytheville, her local reputation was clearly established. Few people knew or cared that she had not completed the requirements at the conservatory. Just by attending that prestigious school she had become a celebrity in her own way, and after only a month or so at home she started teaching piano in Aunt Clara's sunny parlor.

During the next year the number of students wanting to take lessons from the popular piano teacher increased to the point where Fayetta felt she was imposing on Aunt Clara by keeping the parlor occupied so much of the time. As a matter of fact, Aunt Clara's attitude and some of the remarks she made just within Fayetta's hearing suggested she was of the same opinion.

Fortunately for all, an opening for a piano teacher in the Montcrief Consolidated School System was brought to Fayetta's attention. She easily got the job and on the last day of August 1930 moved into the teachers' home.

In the fall of 1938 Rupert Armstrong was hired to teach mathematics and history in the Montcrief High School and took up residency also in the teachers' home. He was unmarried and not glad of it. He found Fayetta appealing and she found his company enjoyable once she had permitted him to see her on a periodic basis. But she was wary, even fearful of fostering any human relationship beyond a certain point, a point beyond which disaster and loss must surely wait to destroy her.

In retrospect, the deaths of her parents and Uncle Lester, which at the time she had miraculously been able to bear, later assumed new significance and horror. How could she have reconciled so soon to the loss of the three people she loved most in the world? Surely she could not so easily cope with such loss now. During the days immediately following her uncle's death, she had ceremoniously laid the cornerstone of the fortress that would henceforth shield her from that specific kind of hurt. To her satisfaction, at least, the fortress had been completed some time ago and the moat bridge drawn and secured. As she had become more fully aware of her vulnerability, she had inventoried herself in meticulous detail, had at one point deliberately sifted out thoughts and feelings that could entrap her and in their stead had devised new responses, new preferences, and new, restricted limits to their exercise.

By summer of 1941 a number of structural flaws in Fayetta's well-planned fortress began to show themselves. For a period of several weeks during sleepless nights she had made attempts of diminishing strength to avert the imminent collapse of her citadel. It was a contest unlike any she'd ever participated in before. The single feature that set this situation apart was her abated efforts to win it. This time, ironically, though it took her a while to face up to it, she desired rather than dreaded defeat.

Three days before the Thanksgiving holidays of 1941, when for at least the tenth time Rupert Armstrong asked her to marry him, she agreed. The wedding was set for the following June.

As soon as war was declared in December, even before Rupert was called into service, Fayetta was convinced she had made a mistake and that the very thing she feared the most—the loss of one she loved—was imminent. But now there was no way to turn back, even if she had wanted to. Not only had she promised him she would marry him; she had already made him a part of her life as surely as her parents and Uncle Lester had been. The wonderful commitment had brought with it a surprising amount of courage and hope.

If there had been any doubts about her feelings for Rupert before he left, the long, lonely months before he returned in 1945 dispelled them. They were married in March and on the twenty-fifth of April, after the last of her three student recitals, she quit teaching at her husband's request and became a full-time wife at 206 Holly Street, Montcrief, Arkansas.

Rupert was made principal of Montcrief High School in May, at about the same time Fayetta Rose Ramsey Armstrong became aware of her impending motherhood. Annette was born in February of the following year. It was without a doubt the happiest single day of Fayetta's life.

On a November night in 1956, while returning with four other teachers from a convention in Little Rock, Rupert was killed instantly in a head-on collision just seven miles from home.

After it was all over, after the first excruciating moments and the ensuing days of shock, disbelief, and anger, Fayetta slowly and oddly felt her own life returning. Trance-like, she saw herself outside herself, some obscure, amorphous object with movement but without direction, seeking a place to rest. She was not consciously aware that in her abject state she actually beckoned to it and wanted it to return.

She watched her precious daughter with intensified, exaggerated love and concern. Annette was now her only reason for living. Annette had been devastated by her father's death but with the strength and resiliency of youth had made a comparatively quick recovery. This sometimes puzzled her mother, who felt in a way that Annette's adjustment indicated she had not loved her father enough. In time, as she became better able to think rationally, she realized her suspicions were baseless and that Annette had some special capacity to put herself and her previously shattered world back together.

Annette was a popular child. After school and on weekends her friends were in and out of the house or she was visiting them or with them at movies or on their bikes. Fayetta naturally felt better when Annette's friends were visiting her. It was much less lonely, the absence of Rupert a little less painful.

In time she realized how therapeutic it was to busy herself in the kitchen, making cookies, candy, and many previously untried refreshments for them. The children brought infectious energy, enthusiasm, and, most of all, youth. Fayetta often observed them eating or playing and took comfort in knowing those dear children would be around tomorrow and for years of tomorrows to come. They were hope. They, like Arkansas spring, the season she loved most, symbolized life's beginning, not its end. More and more she planned activities involving them and sought every inconspicuous means possible to share in their bright and relatively uncomplicated lives.

Annette's eleventh birthday in February 1957 provided the first such opportunity. After some misgiving, Fayetta decided to give her a party. It was a grey, rainy, and cold afternoon with muddy footprints and dripping umbrellas all over the house. Fayetta and Annette had decorated the living room with crepe paper streamers, candles, and an assortment of florist flowers. The commotion, restricted mostly to the living room, was at a high peak. Fayetta, when not supervising the games, was supervising Sophronia, her part-time housekeeper, in the kitchen. Together they were putting the final touches on the refreshments. Sophronia, amused and delighted, was pouring green punch into festive paper cups and Fayetta was spacing the eleven green candles on the three-layered chocolate birthday cake. Suddenly someone began picking out random notes on the piano. This was followed a moment or two later by a fast, clumsy duet of "Chopsticks," screams, and laughter.

In a way it was like a voice from another world, of one dearly loved and too long away. Fayetta straightened without turning from the cake, put her hands to her chin and pressed hard. It was as though some inner source had activated every nerve and sent a burning flood of light and life over every inch of her body.

"Oh Sophronia, listen!" She smiled, then tightened her lips and put a hand over her mouth as she felt the tears overflowing her eyes.

At that moment, while she stood transfixed before her daughter's birthday cake, she realized that what she was feeling was the ultimate if not the only real happiness she would ever know. Her otherwise lonely house was alive now, filled with the voices and laughter and youth of children, like timeless Spring, and the off-pitch sounds of her long-neglected piano.

The aftermath of the birthday party was greatly amplified silence and fiercely accelerated inactivity. That night she lay awake past midnight, long after she had read her Bible and commended her body and soul to God's keeping. The first hour or so she had relived the excitement of the party, recalling everything. She especially remembered the piano playing and her surprise and the wonderful feeling she had had. The piano was so out of tune! Maybe she should call Mr. Glendennin soon and have him tune it. . . . Yes, she would. Maybe tomorrow.

She was innervated to the point where sleep was not possible. She listened to the periodic creaking sounds the house made as it grumpily adjusted to the changing temperature, and the relentless, low humming of the electric alarm clock to her right. Farther away, yet now amply audible, was the irregular dripping of water from the faucets in the kitchen and the bathroom, a routine precaution on very cold nights to prevent the pipes from freezing.

Now at two o'clock she was still awake. The glass of warm milk she had drunk an hour earlier had not helped. Many times before, especially when she was a young girl, she had lain awake, listening as she was doing now, frightened by the stark reality ordinary things assumed in the defenseless, uncamouflaged hours of night. It was a time when one who is alone may be assaulted by thoughts of all that's dreadful, whether inevitable or imagined, thoughts which penetrate the brain undeterred and flaunt their ugly nudity like perverts before someone whose feet are nailed to the floor.

Then, in utter hopelessness, she prayed that she might know what to do. She pulled the covers closer about her face and felt the friendly warmth of the electric blanket. Then she cried. Quietly.

When the alarm clock made its first uncertain, labored sound and then buzzed her to consciousness, she was not aware that she had been asleep. The clearer signal the clock gave seemed to be but a continuation of the incessant drone she had listened to all night. Yet, as her mind adjusted to the light and sounds around her, she realized she had slept briefly after all. She got up feeling unusually good.

On her way to the dining room to raise the thermostat, she passed the piano and sensed immediately that something was different. The lid was up and the keyboard open. She had forgotten to close it last night before going to bed. It had been so long since she'd had to think about that. Such a small matter! Later, after she'd gotten Annette off to school and was having the first of her usual three cups of coffee, vivid thoughts of Aunt Clara vied with happy thoughts of Annette's birthday party for her attention. Even though she hadn't seen Aunt Clara since Rupert's funeral, she felt strangely that she had. And recently. Then all at once she realized she had indeed dreamed of her aunt during the short sleep early this morning. She had been teaching piano again in her aunt's parlor, yet the house was not in Blytheville but in Montcrief. Uncle Lester, too, had been in the dream. He was principal of Montcrief High School and was living in the teachers' home. Remembering the dream made her sweetly sad yet gave her a warm and beautiful feeling.

She poured herself another cup of coffee and walked over to the window. After a cold week or more of low, dark clouds and chilling rain, everything that had survived seemed to be exulting in the sun's return. The bird bath was frozen solid, but the icicles that had formed from the overflow were slowly melting from the warmth of the sun. Her spirit, too, was exulting in the new day.

She went into the living room and stood looking at the piano. She smiled as she remembered hearing it yesterday afternoon. She pulled a volume of Heller studies from the mahogany music cabinet and laid it on the piano under her coffee cup. She sat down with one hand covering the other and watched for a moment or two as the graceful, coffee-scented vapors spiraled upward from the cup and disintegrated in the air. She extended her fingers, then opened and closed them several times. They were so stiff! Tenderly she adjusted her wedding ring. Slowly, cautiously she placed her hands on the keys and began to play a few random chords and fragments of pieces she still remembered. She finished her coffee and for a while sat in a state of near-ecstasy. The moment her fingers had begun to find their way over the yellowed keys she had felt again a joy and peace which only her piano playing could give her. All the persistent, conflicting forces which had plagued her for months were dispelled instantly and relinquished their hold on her soul.

And while she reveled in the return of this misplaced part of her life, she knew that surely she must nurture it again. She must return to teaching. She would share her music with the children; they would share their youth with her.

She ran to the phone and dialed her neighbor, Mabel Paradine. "Good mornin', Mabel. Did I wake you up?"

Mabel gave a boisterous laugh. "Good Lord, Etta, you know better than that. As a matter of fact, Ernest has just left for the office and I'm sittin' here drinkin' coffee all by myself." There was a momentary pause and the sound of a deep swallow of coffee. "What's wrong? Anything the matter, Etta?"

Fayetta gave a little chuckle. "Well, Mabel, the strangest thing has just happened and I'm dyin' to talk with you about it. Do you have time to talk?"

"You know I do, Etta Armstrong. But not on the phone. It sounds to me like if we don't talk you gonna bust a gasket. You sound pos'tively beside yourself. Wrap yourself up real good, Etta, and come on over. I'm gonna pour you a cup of pipin' hot coffee right this minute."

The heavy knocking on the front door shattered her reverie. It must be Sophronia. She folded the sheet of stationery and placed it gently inside the desk drawer. She would need to get her thoughts together before trying to write the letter to Annette. . . . Maybe tonight.

3

ONE OF THE FIRST THINGS MISS ETTA learned about teaching piano was that you teach your best students last whenever possible. She had scheduled Friday afternoon lessons for four of her best students in such a way that she could give them extra time if she wanted to. She felt the good students deserved additional time and, if her regular schedule didn't permit her to keep them over, she very often gave them extra lessons.

Each Friday afternoon at three o'clock, Monica and Mark Mayfield were dropped off by their mother and picked up at four-thirty when and if, during that time, she could do all the things she saved up to do.

Mark, who was eight years old, had his lesson first, while Monica sat in the kitchen or on the back porch, reading one of the many library books she consumed each week, writing poems, or drawing pictures of pretty little girls, all looking the same and wearing all the latest fashions. While Monica was having her lesson, Mark was either reading comic books or outside chasing lizards or harassing the squirrels. When both were done with their lessons, Miss Etta inevitably called them into the kitchen, seated them ceremoniously at the table, and almost always said, "Now, then, because you've both done so well for Miss Etta today, we're gonna have us a little party to celebrate before mother gets back." She would then bring out an assortment of cookies on a tray which had been covered with a starched white napkin, a little bowl of nuts, and three glasses for their Cokes. The glasses, decorated with cartoon characters, had been bought especially for her students. Each was then passed a napkin which also had a cartoon character on it.

Their lessons and the little party were over and still their mother hadn't come to get them. Miss Etta suddenly remembered that she wasn't sure about some of the titles and composers of the pieces they were going to play on their auditions next week, so she got her record book from the living room and had them help her check the information which she would transfer this weekend to the Guild report cards.

This done, she suggested they sit on the front porch and enjoy the nice weather. Monica sat in one of the chairs beside Miss Etta, but Mark preferred to throw rocks at one of Mabel Paradine's cats.

"Mark Mayfield, you stop that!" Monica shouted. "Why do you have to be so mean to that poor cat?" Then to Miss Etta with exasperation, "He's always gettin' into some kind of trouble, Miss Etta. I have to keep an eye on him all the time." You could tell she got a certain satisfaction out of her responsibility.

It was at that very moment that Mabel drove into her driveway and hurriedly got out of the car with a bag of groceries in one hand and her purse in the other. Mark suddenly assumed an air of innocence and pretended to be looking for four-leaf clovers.

Mabel waved with her purse and said she'd had to run to the store for some last-minute things for her company. Her brother Carl, his wife Ethel, and Ethel's old maid sister Isabel Potter were coming to supper.

Miss Etta asked Monica to show her some of her drawings. She had just opened her sketchpad when Velma Mayfield drove up in her big Buick.

The children ran to the car and got in. Miss Etta went around to talk to Velma. Velma patted her hand gently and apologized for being so late. "Did the kids have good lessons today?"

Miss Etta looked over to both of them and smiled. "They always have good lessons, Velma. They're my little star pupils. You should be very proud of them."

Velma reached over and patted each of them on the head. "Well, I reckon I am . . . sorta. . . . Now about the auditions, Miss Etta. Have you told them exactly what to do and when to be at the church?"

"Yes, I've written everything down in their assignment books. I'd like for them to be at the church at least fifteen minutes before their auditions just in case Mr. Riddick runs ahead of time. I don't think he's apt to, but it's always a good idea to be early. I'd hate to make him wait around."

"Okay then, that's settled. I'll see to it that they're at the church in plenty of time." Then she paused. "Oh, Miss Etta, I was wonderin' if you'd like to ride over to Little Rock with Vern and me and the kids tomorrow. We're going over to get Monica a dress for the recital and thought we'd eat lunch and just sorta make a day of it."

"Oh Velma, I don't think so. I've got tons of things to do before the auditions, and I've also got to teach Myrtle Prenshaw's Sunday School class. But thanks anyway. I do appreciate it."

Velma took one of Miss Etta's hands and squeezed it. "Miss Etta, you always say that. I know you've got lots of things to do, but it'd do you so much good to get out of the house for a bit. And we'd really love to have you along. Please, won't you say yes?"

She got that far-away look in her eyes. Deep down inside, she knew how much she would enjoy going with them, but the instinctive reaction was always the same, to say no and then retreat into her private world once her teaching was done.

Velma put her head out the window and gently kissed her on the cheek. "We love you, Miss Etta. . . . Now look, we don't plan on leavin' till around ten o'clock, so if in the meantime you change your mind, just give me a call, hear?"

"All right, Velma, and thanks again. It's mighty sweet of you to ask me. Bye-bye now."

She rocked in her chair on the porch and thought about how

she would spend her evening after the next students were gone. She should try again to write Annette, and she should at least begin filling out the thirty-two Guild cards. It took so long now to write all that information by hand. She'd see how she felt later before deciding what to do.

She heard the loose sidewalk slab and looked up.

"Hello, Miss Etta," Mollie Hong called cheerfully as she approached the porch. She was walking briskly and erect, as usual, carrying her vinyl music case pressed to her heart and a little bouquet of sweet peas in her hand. Her long, straight, black hair flowed down and bounced about her back and cascaded over her shoulders like an uncontained waterfall overflowing its banks and playing toss and catch with the sun.

"Hello, Mollie dear. I see you're walkin' today. How come?"

Mollie came up on the porch, smiling and throwing her head back as though she were modeling. "I wanted to because it's so pretty. Isn't the weather wonderful? I've been beside myself all day." She reached down, gave the sweet peas to Miss Etta, and patted her hand. "Here. These are for you. . . . And how are you, Miss Etta?"

She got up and put her arm around Mollie's waist. "I'm just fine, dear. And thank you for the lovely flowers. You're so sweet to bring them to me. . . . Mollie, you look so happy."

She put her arm around Miss Etta's waist. "That's because I am."

Miss Etta looked at the sweet peas and smiled wistfully. "I've always loved sweet peas, Mollie. You can't imagine how much. When I was a girl and used to play on recitals, we always had big baskets and vases of sweet peas all over the stage. To this very day, whenever I see or smell sweet peas, it reminds me of my childhood."

Mollie had gathered up her music and was ready to leave when Miss Etta asked her if she'd like a glass of Coke before going home. She declined graciously. She needed to get on home because she was walking and had to help her mother with supper when she got home. Miss Etta told her about being a little early for her audition and to make sure she got a good night's sleep the night before.

After Mollie left, she walked down the sidewalk to get her newspaper, rolled and rubber-banded, in the ditch. She opened it and slipped the rubber band around her wrist. As she scanned the front page, she saw Mabel, all dressed up, standing at her front door. Mabel waved feebly. Each Friday at six o'clock, she could be seen at some little job in the yard, feeding her cats, or just sitting on the porch. She always stopped whatever she was doing when Gamaliel Barrett's mother drove up and let him out for his lesson.

Mrs. Barrett would never come inside the house or even sit on the front porch while Gamaliel was having his lesson, even though Miss Etta had often invited her to. Instead, she would sit in the car, an old rebuilt Pontiac with dents and scratches and a worn set of tires. She sometimes brought some sewing, read magazines, or shelled peas or beans. When it was too cold to sit in the car, she would drive up town and do some shopping. She often smiled, but sometimes it was hard to know if she really meant it. Even when the smile seemed genuine, it looked sad, as though the smiling action had been put to a vote and most of the muscles involved had said yes, while some still said no.

Ten-year-old Gamaliel, though uninhibited by comparison with his mother, seemed, nevertheless, to be always under her remote control. He was good-looking, neat, and polite. He was also very talented. His talent was so remarkable that Miss Etta had offered in the beginning to teach him without charge. Mrs. Barrett had been appreciative but had kindly declined the offer. Nor would she agree to a reduction in the fee.

Gamaliel would be playing his first audition this year and was looking forward to it as much as his older brother was looking forward to the next baseball game. Today, Miss Etta had him do everything just as he would do it on his audition.

As she watched his small hands move rapidly and securely over the keys, her pleasure increased measurably. She thought of the first lessons and her private misgivings about their relationship. She still remembered with secret shame the first time she had put her hand on his to show him how to relax his wrist. It had been a spontaneous gesture on her part, as with any other student, yet the contact had chilled her and made her withdraw her hand as quickly and inconspicuously as possible. Then she had sat for a distracted minute or two, trying to think rationally about what she had done and felt. For a number of days following that incident, she had pondered it and finally admitted to herself that she had been mean, ugly, and unfair. His hand had felt like any other student's hand.

As he gathered up his music and put it back into the book sack, she said, "Now you wait right here while I run back to the kitchen. I wanna give you some cookies to take home. Would you like that?"

He said he would but seemed uncomfortable about it.

As they walked to the car, she placed her hand lightly on his shoulder. She opened the door for him to get in, then went around to the other side to talk with his mother.

At that point, Mrs. Barrett quickly returned her sewing to the basket beside her on the seat. She smiled. "How'd he do, Miz Armstrong?"

She put both hands on the car door and for an awkward moment wanted to reach inside and touch her. Instead, she leaned forward. "He did just beautifully, Mrs. Barrett. Gamaliel's gonna play a fine audition. We don't have a thing to worry about."

She seemed pleased and reached over to pat Gamaliel's hand. "Dat's good. We takes yo' wuhd fo' it." She looked ready to go. As she put her hand to the ignition key, she knocked the basket with the sewing onto the floor. She hastily picked it up and replaced it beside her. Gamaliel watched with concern. Miss Etta pretended not to have noticed. She told Mrs. Barrett that she'd written all the information about the audition in Gamaliel's assignment book and had scheduled his audition for the afternoon so they'd have plenty of time to drive over from Milam. Mrs. Barrett thanked her with a sad smile and said she'd have him there early and would see that he practiced hard.

It was a few minutes past seven when she finally ended her teaching day. Before she did anything else, she locked the front door, then checked to see that the back door also was locked. Sometimes she'd forget to lock the back door after Sophronia had left it open. As she moved about the house, she felt relieved that her teaching week was over. It had been more strenuous than usual. It always was more strenuous just before competitions and recitals. Nevertheless, she knew that just below her consciousness there was a trap door that could spring open in an instant if she didn't watch out. At ordinary times, she could forget about the trap door and project herself into the future, if for only an hour or so, and avoid the abyss it so weakly concealed. Even now she made a special effort to keep busy.

She ate a bowl of cereal, then sat in her favorite bedroom chair to read the paper. Some of what she read made her uneasy. There had been a series of attacks on older women during the past several months. She had worried about this threat for a long time, but had been able so far to put it in perspective, just as she could sometimes put the trap door in perspective. But reading the hideous details in the paper caused a renewed and strengthened horror.

There was also an account of a tornado that had completely destroyed a small Oklahoma town only yesterday. The picture accompanying the article showed several bewildered families, some searching through the remains of their homes and others trying to comfort one another. She didn't want to read about it. Because such stories always sickened her and threatened to crack the wall she'd put between herself and the tragedy she'd suffered as a child, she had never since that time let herself read anything about tornadoes. She couldn't help reading a few words, however, as she covered the picture with both hands. The picture and the few words that had jumped out at her suddenly heightened her distress. With the newspaper spread open across her lap, she sat motionless, all her thoughts racing in reverse. . . . But she must not think about that long ago event! She would make herself think of something else. . . . The auditions!

Now that her students had played their last lessons before the auditions, she was able to make rational assessments of their capabilities and needs. This reminded her of the Guild cards and the tedious work they would require. . . . But not tonight. That would just have to wait until tomorrow. . . . Maybe the Sunday School lesson. That would put her thoughts back on the right track. . . . But no, not even that could interest her now. She knew the longer she sat idle, the greater the danger of becoming depressed.

With an attempted enthusiasm, she got up, collected the Guild cards and her record book, and sat down at her desk. As she sat down, she could see Mabel and her guests. They must have just finished eating and were about to clear the table. She watched for a minute or two. She managed to fill out ten of the thirty-two cards, then put everything aside. She'd finish them tomorrow.

Tomorrow! How close it was and how long it was going to be! What would she do? How could she pass the time until Sunday, when she'd go to church, eat lunch with a few of the members of her Sunday School class, and then look forward to Monday and the auditions? She remembered Velma Mayfield's invitation to go to Little Rock. The thought was a brightening one, yet she still felt very reluctant to call Velma.

Velma and the mothers of some of her other students posed the greatest present threat to the tenuous balance she was trying to maintain between personal involvement and aloofness with adults and contemporaries. Being as fond of Velma as she was, she could so easily become dependent upon her, and the next thing she knew, she'd be trapped again.

Like the doors of her house in winter, there were two doors to her sequestered world—a regular wooden one which was always there to be used under normal conditions, and a stronger, steel-reinforced storm door which was hung when conditions were more severe. The storm door of her house was put on and taken off seasonally; the storm door to her private life was never removed.

Yet it seemed that lately it had been more and more difficult to keep the storm door shut. She often found herself tottering on the edge of an abyss, ready to say yes to a social invitation that would put her with others her own age. The frequency and intensity of her periods of depression had perceptibly increased. She tried to understand why this change in her outlook had come about so drastically.

She thought about how often her memory had failed her lately. Three or four times during the past week, she had forgotten to do things she was supposed to do. And even though nobody else knew about it, she still reddened and wanted to cry when she remembered how, just a week or so ago, she had put her car keys in the refrigerator and couldn't find them for several days. And just yesterday she had to be reminded that she was supposed to teach Myrtle Prenshaw's Sunday School class. . . . Now she was touching all the sore spots.

She took her wedding picture from the dresser and held it with both trembling hands. In the bright lamp light she could see the dust and an accumulation of finger prints on it. She wiped the glass with her handkerchief, then sat down on the edge of the bed. How seldom she had allowed herself to ponder the transformation that had taken place since that picture was made! She rarely let herself assess the deterioration or measure the nearly measureless time remaining before the end. Looking at the picture had a distressing effect. When she finally put it back and stood at the window, she felt incorporeal. She was not here. She was still in that picture. She had already died.

If not, then how would she die? How would it actually happen? . . . When, and how soon? . . . She walked about the room, touching her face and hair, then putting one hand on top of the other to scrutinize them, holding them close to her eyes and trying to hypnotize herself back into herself the scary way she used to do as a young girl. . . . It didn't work anymore.

What if she were to have a stroke, a heart attack, or some other kind of accident and nobody knew about it? She knew of several people who had been found days after they'd died. . . . Just across the street, Rowena Dobbins! . . . Who would find her? Or, worse still, what if she had to be put in a nursing home? A nursing home where she and all the other lonely old people could watch one another die.

Before she realized fully what she was doing, she picked up the phone and called Velma. The line was busy. While she waited before calling again, she stood at her window and looked over to where

Mabel, Carl, Ethel, and Isabel were sitting on the porch in the waning daylight. Carl was talking and gesturing with his hands while Mabel rocked in the swing, her feet never touching the floor. Ethel was flipping through a magazine and straining to see. Isabel sat erect and humorless in a rocker and looked passively into the distance.

She jumped when the phone rang. It was Mrs. Harrison, calling to ask about Jennifer's audition. Miss Etta told her the information was in Jennifer's assignment book. Mrs. Harrison said it wasn't.

"Oh dear!" she sighed. "Did I forget to write it down for her?"

"You must have, Miss Etta, 'cause I don't see it anywhere."

She looked at her schedule and told Mrs. Harrison what she wanted to know. Mrs. Harrison thanked her and was about to hang up when Miss Etta remembered several other things Jennifer should know. But she didn't stop. One thing led to another and Mrs. Harrison finally said if she thought of anything else she'd call back.

She called Velma again but got no answer. She walked distractedly from one room to another. In the dining room, she stopped to look at the sweet peas Mollie had brought her. She bent down to smell them. The subtle fragrance instantly triggered a thousand happy thoughts of her youth, thoughts made happier, in retrospect, by her present discontent. Sweet peas symbolized all the past Aprils of her life. Now, more than ever before, they represented the abbreviated spring of her life, those few precious years when Rupert was alive and Annette was a child experiencing her own first springs. She moved the vase of flowers into her bedroom. As she placed them on the bedside table, she took Rupert's picture and looked at it. She felt herself slipping. She went again to her desk to fill out some more cards. As she moved things from one side to the other, she knocked over the little brass letter rack that Monica Mayfield had given her last Christmas and which she used for unanswered mail. Annette's letter was on top. She opened it with misgiving and read it twice. When she finished, she pressed it between her hands and tried bravely but without success to keep from crying. She sobbed, "Oh, dear God! Dear God!" The flood gates gave way and her small body convulsed in despair.

4

THE SIDEWALKS OF DOWNTOWN MONTCRIEF were nearly deserted, but the streets were alive with early morning traffic as Miss Etta slowly made her way to the First Baptist Church in her blue Ford. It was Monday, the first day of the Guild auditions. As chairperson of the local chapter, she must see that everything goes smoothly and that the judge is comfortable and furnished with all the things he needs to do his job. In addition to those items of necessity, she had beside her on the seat and on the floor several trays of cookies, cupcakes, and candy, and a large jug of punch. These things were for the students after they played their auditions and for the judge when he took his periodic breaks.

As predicted, the weather had changed. The dirty grey sky looked and felt only tree-top high, and the humidity seemed thick enough to slice. The clouds were in a constant state of movement, allowing the sun to appear from time to time to add more sultry heat to the adhesive humidity. There was not even a single breeze to alleviate the debilitating atmosphere. Miss Etta, who normally felt the heat less than others, was feeling it now. She dabbed her handkerchief occasionally at her forehead and upper lip. This certainly put a damper on the excitement that usually characterized the Guild auditions.

It was only seven-thirty. She would have an hour to set things up before the auditions began. Mr. Riddick would probably arrive shortly. He had called last night from the motel to let her know he'd arrived and to confirm the audition schedule. Virgiline Canfield, whose students would play first, was waiting outside the church when Miss Etta pulled up into the parking lot. The church was locked and Miss Etta had the key.

"Mornin', Virgiline," she said as she got out of the car. "Could you help me haul some of this stuff inside?"

The students would sit in a small room down the hall from where the auditions would be held. Just off this room was a small kitchen where they put the refreshments. Another teacher, Willie Belle Hawkins, was supposed to bring a bag of ice before things got underway.

Miss Etta felt better once she was inside the church. In fact, she was as excited as she could be. She and Virgiline moved a table into the choir room where the students would play, turned the big upright piano around so the judge could see the students' hands, and laid out a supply of sharpened pencils, pens, and paper, and a little brass bell for Mr. Riddick to ring when he was ready for the next student. Miss Etta managed to find an old rag under the kitchen sink and gave the piano a good going-over. When she finished, she ran her fingers over the keys and was startled to hear how badly out of tune the piano was. And to make matters even worse, the action was faulty and several keys stuck. This embarrassed her and caused a great deal of concern since it was bound to affect the way the students played. She hadn't realized how bad the piano was. Sylvia Myers, the choir director, had told her the piano had just been tuned. How she wished they could use the new Japanese grand in the sanctuary! She hadn't asked to use it because she didn't feel the sanctuary was an appropriate place to hold the auditions. She walked around the room for a while and finally decided the best thing to do was to apologize beforehand to Mr. Riddick and hope for the best.

Willie Belle Hawkins arrived with the ice, blowing her breath upward from her extended bottom lip in an effort to cool the upper part of her face. "Merciful Father, isn't this humidity awful!" Then, as she put the ice into the small refrigerator, "Have you got everything under control, Etta?"

"I think so, thanks to Virgiline's help. But goodness gracious alive! Have y'all tried the piano in the choir room? It's in deplorable shape."

They went and tried it and agreed it was bad.

"What I hate most is how it's gonna affect the students," Miss Etta said. "But I'm also worried about what Mr. Riddick will think."

Virgiline shrugged her shoulders. "I'm sure he's heard worse, Etta. And as for how it'll affect my students, I don't think it's gonna make a bit of difference. They wouldn't play any better if they had a brand new Steinway."

"Why Virgiline, you oughta be ashamed of yourself!" Miss Etta said. "You know that's not true."

"Wanna bet? You just wait'n see. About this time every year, I get so fed up with 'em I could strangle every last one of 'em."

Willie Belle laughed and reached over and took a cookie from one of the trays. "I hope you don't mind, Etta. I didn't have any breakfast yet."

Miss Etta still looked worried. She looked at her watch and then out the window that faced the parking lot.

Willie Belle tossed the crumbs from her cookie into the waste basket and reached down to smooth her stockings. "Etta, I know you're upset about the piano, but I think you're makin' too much over it. Most of these kids have pianos that are worse than this one. And some of 'em don't even have a piano. And, remember, it'll be just as fair for one as the other."

"Oh, Willie Belle, I don't agree. I think we owe it to these children to make things as convenient as possible so they can play their very best." She turned back to the window.

Willie Belle took another cookie, this time from a different tray. "Well, whether you agree or not, Etta, this ain't a contest, you know. These kids aren't competin' against each other, and there aren't any prizes. I think the only thing that matters is that they have the experience of playin' and gettin' as much fun as possible from it. I think you're much too serious about the whole thing. You always have been."

Miss Etta didn't respond. She always disagreed with Willie Belle about teaching. In knowledgeable circles, Willie Belle's students were not highly regarded. Elsewhere, it didn't seem to matter. She had more students than any other teacher, partly because she also taught voice, violin, trumpet, and saxophone. She had been a home economics major in college and had minored in music because she'd always liked to fool around with several instruments and enjoyed singing pop music a lot. She had graduated from college feeling she was fully qualified to teach any of the instruments she played. She often remarked that a teacher didn't need to know how to perform well on an instrument in order to teach it. Especially to beginners. While the quality of her teaching disproved that theory, her popularity and the diversity of her students seemed to support it. She made sure she attended every workshop within commuting distance and that this fact was promptly reported in the *Montcrief Herald*.

"It's eight-twenty-five, and I'm gettin' worried," Miss Etta said as she looked out the window and again at her watch.

Virgiline put her arm around Miss Etta's shoulders. "Relax, Etta. Everything's gonna work out just fine. He'll be here, just wait and see. And so what if he's a little late? It won't really matter."

The door at the end of the hall slammed them to attention. It was Pamela Murphy and her mother. Pam was the first of Virgiline's students to play. After Virgiline hugged her and made a lot over her pretty outfit, Miss Etta suggested that Pam go into the choir room and try the piano out before the judge came.

"Just look at all that food!" Eunice Murphy crowed as she went around lifting the cloths covering the trays of goodies. "All this food and not a drop of coffee!" she added, looking at the empty coffee maker on the counter.

Miss Etta slapped her thighs. "Oh, my goodness! I simply forgot all about the coffee." She took the carafe and filled it with water.

"Etta, let me do that. You've done enough." Virgiline started opening cabinet doors, looking for the coffee.

"I think they keep it in the refrigerator," Willie Belle said.

Some sound drew Miss Etta's attention to the parking lot. She hurried over to the window. "Oh, he's here! That's Mr. Riddick, y'all! Oh, thank goodness!" She looked at her watch again, then tugged nervously at her skirt.

The others ran over to look. Mr. Riddick was locking his car. He opened his briefcase, put something in it, then closed it. As he walked across the parking lot to the church, he checked the knot of his tie and centered it.

"I can't believe it!" Eunice said.

"I thought the only place you found men like that was in Hollywood," Willie Belle said, laughing. She bent over and straightened her stockings.

Miss Etta hurried down the hall to meet him, touching the fingers of her right hand to her hair and making little nervous sounds in her throat.

"Mr. Riddick, I'm Fayetta Armstrong." She extended a soft, weak hand.

He shook it and smiled. "I'm very happy to meet you, Mrs. Armstrong. I feel I already know you. . . . I apologize for being late. I had a little car trouble."

As they walked down the hall, she said it really didn't matter and she hoped the trouble wasn't serious. She put a hand to the back of her hair and gave a little cough.

In the choir room, she asked if things were the way he liked, and when he assured her they were, she pointed out that the piano was not in very good condition and that there was a bathroom just outside that door there to his right.

Pam Murphy stood by the piano, not knowing what to do. Miss Etta walked over and put her arm around her. "Pam, honey, I think Mr. Riddick would like a little time to get organized. So in the meantime, let's you and I go back where Mother and Mrs. Canfield are."

Mr. Riddick was laying out his materials. He propped the blue score card against his briefcase where he could easily refer to it. "I'm really sorry, Mrs. Armstrong. I'll just be a minute or two."

When she returned to the kitchen, Virgiline, Willie Belle, and Eunice were like three giddy school girls.

"Oh Etta, tell us what he looks like up close," Eunice said.

Miss Etta blushed and tugged at her skirt. "Why Eunice, you embarrass me!"

Virgiline laughed into her coffee cup. "He's a sight better lookin' than old Mr. Scanlan last year. Remember that poor old soul?"

"Virgiline, shame on you! Mr. Scanlan was a very kind man," Miss Etta said. "And remember, handsome is as handsome does. Let's just hope Mr. Riddick's judgin' is as commendable as his looks are."

Eunice and Willie Belle looked at each other and laughed. Eunice slapped Willie Belle's arm. "At this stage of the game who's concerned about his judgin' anyway!"

Miss Etta was thoroughly embarrassed and distracted. The sound of the little bell brought her back. "Oh Virgiline, he's ready! Where's Pam?"

Virgiline put her coffee cup down. "Pam? Where's Pam Murphy?" She went into the other room. "Oh, there you are." She straightened the little girl's collar and gave her a tender hug of encouragement. "Okay, Pam, it's time. . . . Now you just relax and go in there and do your very best and don't worry about a thing, hear? . . . D'you feel all right, honey?"

"Yessum, I reckon."

While Pamela was playing her audition and the four women drank coffee and tried to keep their voices down, Willie Belle suggested they take Mr. Riddick out to lunch. Miss Etta let the idea register before she spoke. "Where do you think we should take him?"

"Well, that depends on how much time we've got," Virgiline answered. "How much time does the schedule allow for lunch?"

Miss Etta took her copy from the folder. "An hour and a half," she said. "But we started late, and that's gonna make us run even later."

Willie Belle took another cookie. "Oh, I'm sure he'll catch up, especially if he knows we're takin' him out to eat. After all, what difference does it make if we take a few minutes extra to eat?"

Miss Etta was overly conscientious about her responsibilities and was always reluctant to change the schedule sent by the Guild. The thought, however, was such a nice and generous one. After all, judges had to pay their own room and board out of what they made. "I believe we can work it out," she said finally.

"Okay, that's fine!" Willie Belle said. "Now where to? . . . How 'bout us takin' him to Bonelli's? I bet he likes I-talian food."

Miss Etta wasn't fond of Italian food herself but knew there'd be other things she could eat. "I think that's a good idea. Is that all right with you, Virgiline?"

Virgiline said it was. She was easy to satisfy.

Miss Etta looked very pleased. She said she'd mention it to him when he took his first break at ten-thirty.

Willie Belle said she needed to get home to fix something for Herschel's lunch but would wait until Pam came out to hear what she had to say about Mr. Riddick.

In the meantime, Voncille Baker arrived with her mother, who said she needed to run up town for a few minutes and would pick Voncille up about nine-thirty.

They heard the choir room door slam and waited for Pamela to give an account of her audition.

"How'd you do, Pam?" Virgiline asked as the little girl came into the room and pretended she was going to faint.

She shrugged her shoulders and shook her pony tail. "All right, I reckon."

Mrs. Murphy gave a little grunt. "Is that all you've got to say, Pamela? We knew already you were gonna do all right, but what we wanna know is what you thought of Mr. Riddick. Did you like him? What did he say, honey? Was he very hard?"

Pam would need to wind down before she could answer. "No'm," she said finally, "I didn't think he was hard." Then she squeezed both hands together and gave a big smile. "He was real nice. . . . And real good-lookin'!"

Willie Belle winked at Virgiline. "Yes, honey, we know."

Miss Etta bent over and gently squeezed Pam to her. "I know Pam didn't have any trouble. She's a very fine little student. . . . But tell us, dear, did you have to play all your pieces?"

"Yessum. He asked me to." She looked at her mother and beamed. "Whenever he said anything, he'd smile and sometimes he'd write and talk all at the same time."

They looked at one another. Pamela's account, of course, meant nothing in the long run. They wouldn't be able to evaluate Mr. Riddick's judging until Virgiline got her cards later and they could see what kind of scores he'd given and what comments he'd made. Willie Belle picked up her purse and left, saying she'd be back a little before twelve.

The ringing of the bell meant it was time for Voncille's audition.

5

WILLIE BELLE SUGGESTED THEY GO IN her car since it was bigger than Miss Etta's or Virgiline's. It was a brilliant white Lincoln Continental with every convenience anybody could ever want. She had spruced herself up since earlier this morning and she and Virgiline were waiting for Miss Etta and Mr. Riddick, who were still in the church. Virgiline had just been given her students' report cards and was looking at the scores and reading what Mr. Riddick had written. If the cards held any surprises, they were that the children had done as well as they had. She was satisfied.

It seemed everybody was talking about the weather. On the way to Bonelli's, Willie Belle told them what she'd heard on TV just before leaving the house. A large number of severe thunderstorms with extremely high winds, hail, and lightning were being spawned by the opposing forces of a cold front from the north and a hot and humid one from the gulf. Most of the western part of Arkansas was under a severe weather watch.

Without realizing she was doing so, Miss Etta began to think about her childhood. She wondered if people back then were warned about tornadoes the way they were today. Surely she couldn't remember anything about what happened before the tornado that killed her parents that dreadful night. Only what happened afterwards. And this she must not do! She must pray that there would be no tornadoes. She closed her eyes and sent a few words skyward. She felt better being with other people.

Except for this disturbing news and some occasional uneasiness when Willie Belle expounded her views on teaching, Miss Etta thought the lunch at Bonelli's was a pleasant experience. Willie Belle monopolized the conversation and two or three times tried to solicit some comments from Mr. Riddick about his ideas on piano playing and teaching. He was a superb diplomat, responding each time in such a way that Willie Belle seemed to have trouble understanding exactly what he'd said.

At one point Virgiline asked, "Whose students are playin' this afternoon, Etta?"

Miss Etta had just taken a sip of tea. She wiped her lips and pushed her plate of unfinished food away. "Leigh-Ann Bishop," she replied.

Willie Belle gave a little sneer. "Oh, that one!"

After an awkward moment of silence, Virgiline spoke. "Well, you've got to admit, Willie Belle, her students play awfully well, and she's a fine musician and teacher. . . . I only wish I knew how she does it."

Miss Etta was noticeably embarrassed. She felt it was inappropriate to talk like this in Mr. Riddick's presence. She cleared her throat and made little brush strokes with her fingers on the tablecloth to remove something that wasn't there. She looked at Mr. Riddick. "Mrs. Bishop lives in Gridley, which is about thirty miles from here. She's only bringin' twelve of her students."

Mr. Riddick said he should be getting back to work and thanked them for the delicious lunch. Miss Etta was relieved. They were already over thirty minutes behind schedule. On the way to the car, Willie Belle asked Virgiline if she were satisfied with her students' scores. Miss Etta, also, was curious. Virgiline said she was pleased and had expected much worse.

Leigh-Ann Bishop was standing in the door of the waiting room when Miss Etta and Mr. Riddick returned. Miss Etta introduced her to Mr. Riddick and apologized for being late. Mr. Riddick went directly to the choir room.

Leigh-Ann's twelve students, all neatly dressed and groomed, sat quietly erect, holding their music, precisely organized with numbered strips of paper marking each piece the way it was listed on the report cards. When the bell sounded and the first student went to play, Miss Etta decided to go home for a while. She told Leigh-Ann she'd return later and wanted to show Mr. Riddick some of Montcrief. She asked her to give him some cookies and coffee when he took his break.

It was about four-thirty when she returned. All except two of Leigh-Ann's pupils had played and she was listening for the bell. As soon as it rang and the next student went to play, Miss Etta suggested they go to the kitchen and have a cup of coffee. Leigh-Ann said she was getting sleepy and needed one.

They sat at the kitchen table and inevitably talked about teaching. She told Leigh-Ann she wasn't pleased with the results she'd been getting from most of her students and didn't know what to do about it. Leigh-Ann modestly acknowledged that she, too, was disappointed with her own teaching.

"Oh, for goodness sake, Leigh-Ann," she replied, "your students always do beautifully. You're a splendid teacher. And so young, too. You're an inspiration to me and some others as well."

Leigh-Ann smiled and thanked her. "If my students do well, it's probably because I let only the best ones audition. I have eighteen others who didn't come because they haven't worked hard enough. I consider a competition or an audition a form of reward that students of all ages should aspire to. I realize the Guild feels differently but I can't help it. That's the way I am. Some of my friends tell me occasionally that I'm too idealistic and uncompromising. That always flatters me."

She apologized for monopolizing the conversation, got up and took her cup to the sink and rinsed it out.

"There's no reason to apologize," Miss Etta responded eagerly. "I'm most interested in what you have to say. It all makes such good sense." Yes, she'd heard people like Willie Belle talking about Leigh-Ann's strict teaching methods and, yes, she herself had sometimes questioned them. It was obvious to everyone that Leigh-Ann was a very principled lady and a teacher from whom others could learn a great deal. She washed the two cups, poured out the coffee that was left, and washed the carafe. As she dried her hands, she turned to Leigh-Ann. Her voice was softer now and a little shaky. It was as though she were talking to herself. "I suppose I'm really too old to still be teaching. . . . I realize I'm not as effective as I used to be. I worry sometimes about that. I'm afraid I've become too lenient in my old age."

The bell sounded and Leigh-Ann sent the last student down the hall.

Miss Etta was collecting the left-over refreshments and trays and straightening up the kitchen and the chairs in the waiting room when Mr. Riddick found her half an hour later. Leigh-Ann and her students had just left, obviously pleased with their scores.

Mr. Riddick looked tired, yet he held his tall, slim body erect and managed a pleasant but weary smile when he saw her. She noted that his long, blonde hair was still neatly in place and his tan suit, except for a series of wrinkles at the back of the legs, still looked impeccable. He laid his briefcase down on a chair and took off his coat. She closed some cabinet doors and came back into the waiting room.

When she asked him if he would like to ride around town, he hesitated at first, then said it might be a relaxing diversion. "On one condition," he said. "That we have a cup of coffee first." He had evidently seen the empty carafe on the counter. "Maybe we could stop off somewhere downtown."

"I've got a better idea. If you'll help me haul some of this stuff out to the car, we'll go to my house and have a cup there before doin' our sight-seein'. You can just follow me to the house in your car."

Later, while she made the coffee, he had a look around the living room. When she brought the coffee, he asked who some of the people in the pictures were. She told him, hesitating from time to time when she momentarily lost contact with the present.

"When I was a child, I lived in just such a house as this," he said. "For a while, just now, I forgot where I was." He said he was fond of old homes and that he was fast becoming nostalgic. She gave a little laugh and said she understood.

He scanned the sky to the west as he opened the car door and helped her in. "Looks like what they said about the weather is true. One of the students a while ago said she'd heard a late report that didn't sound very good."

She didn't reply until she'd settled in and checked her face in the mirror. She cleared her throat. "Yes, I'm afraid we're in for it. We have so much bad weather in Arkansas. Do y'all have many tornadoes in Louisiana?"

"Oh yes. Maybe even more than you all do. And don't forget, we also have hurricanes." He saw that she was looking apprehensively to the west before driving off. "Does bad weather frighten you?" he asked.

She answered with a soft, anguished sound. "Very much so. It was because of a tornado that I lost both of my parents when I was a child."

"Oh, I'm so sorry. How terrible! No wonder you're afraid."

She squeezed the steering wheel and was momentarily distracted. In a moment, she turned and gave a little smile. "But that was long, long ago. Are you afraid of bad weather, Mr. Riddick?"

He seemed not to have heard. Then, "Oh, yes. Sometimes."

She knew he was looking at her. She could almost read his mind.

"Does it bother you to talk about it?" he asked finally.

The expression on her face changed as she tried to decide how to answer. "Well, I'm not sure. I haven't talked about it for many years. I've tried to put it out of my mind." She stopped suddenly to wonder if she might be saying too much. Yet she couldn't stop; something was compelling her to keep talking, even though she knew she would regret it later. She cleared her throat. "The only thing is that here lately it seems to be gettin' harder and harder to do. We seem to have so much more bad weather nowadays than we used to."

"It does seem that way. Yet I wonder if perhaps that's because of our highly developed communication media which we didn't have back then. Or at least not to such an extent."

"Perhaps you're right." She gave a soft, low chuckle. "Mr. Riddick, I hope I don't offend you by tellin' you somethin' about my childhood." She hesitated, thinking he might say something, but he didn't. This caused her to question the advisability of pursuing the matter.

He turned suddenly and looked at her. "Oh, I'm sorry," he said. "I was waiting for you to continue. Please do. I'm sure it won't offend me."

It took a few moments for her to recapture her thoughts. "Talkin' about bein' afraid of bad weather, I was gonna tell you how all my classmates used to make fun of me when we'd have bad weather and I'd get sick. You see, I had just been adopted by my Aunt Clara and taken to live with her and my cousins in Blytheville. Pretty soon, all my teachers knew about how scared I'd get, so they did everything they could to keep me from gettin' upset every time it would start thunderin' or lightnin'. At first, I'd even get scared if a dark cloud came up." She stopped and laughed. "After a while I got over some of my fear, but it was very difficult to do. I guess it was easier in a way back then because we didn't have as much bad weather as we have now. Or maybe, as you suggested, we did have but just didn't know about it."

She laughed again, then sobered and fell silent. It occurred to her that she was talking entirely too much about herself yet she seemed unable to stop. The more she talked, the better she felt. It felt strange, however, digging up those old bones. She looked straight ahead, almost heedless of the other automobiles on the road. She turned slightly to see his reaction. He turned and smiled. This was enough to start her talking again.

"I failed to mention that at first I used to get so scared I'd get sick to my stomach. I remember I'd even hide under the bed when we'd have bad weather. That's what—" She broke off abruptly and clutched the steering wheel until her hands went white. She swallowed and coughed several times and her lips trembled. "I thought that was a safe place to be." She gave a right turn signal. "That's where I was the night the tornado killed Mamma and Papa."

He turned to study her face which outwardly, at least, seemed to have assumed a look of serenity. "What a brave little girl you must have been. Surely God spared you because He had other plans for you."

She smiled sadly and nodded her head. "Yes," she said hoarsely. "I used to think that, too. Sometimes, though, I used to wonder about that." Her voice trailed off. Then, with more spirit, "But I'm sure He did. I couldn't have stood it otherwise."

As they turned onto Magnolia Street, a little brown terrier darted out into the street and barely avoided being hit by the car. Miss Etta hadn't noticed. For a few moments, neither of them spoke. Mr. Riddick seemed lost in thought as he watched people mowing or watering their lawns, planting things, or sitting in big rockers on long, wide porches. He turned to face her. She felt him looking at her.

"I'm sorry, Mrs. Armstrong, if talking about your sad experiences upsets you, but I can't seem to get it off my mind. I'm sitting here thinking about how that tornado affected you," he said. "Obviously, it turned your whole life around."

She pondered that for a while. "That's right," she replied softly and turned slowly, cautiously onto the highway. "Tornadoes have a way of doing that. That's the way they are. They either take your life or they turn it around, as you put it. They're unforgettable."

She sniffed a time or two and made a special effort to smile. "Now," she said enthusiastically, "let me show you our fair city of Montcrief!"

Most of the stores had closed and the streets were quiet. Several cars and a long truck were getting or waiting to get gas at the only downtown gas station. She pointed out the garment factory that had given Montcrief a new lease on life back in nineteen forty-eight, and the plant where automobile parts were made by a foreign manufacturer, and the Montcrief Consolidated School System, where she had taught for many years and where she still gave her student recitals. Not far from the school she showed him the newest shopping center, Mont-Mart. It was a busy place with a large supermarket and seven smaller shops.

Farther out, going north, she proudly showed him the newer section of town. A number of beautiful and expensive homes were situated randomly in an expanse of forest which up until a few years ago had never been considered a suitable development site. She explained that most of the people living there were from out of state and worked with the garment factory or the automobile parts plant.

Later, as he was getting ready to leave, he made some comments about her plants on the porch and asked what they were. He said he liked plants and flowers, and she said she would give him some cuttings before he went back to Louisiana. As she was pointing out certain ones and telling him what they were and how and when to plant them, she noticed Mabel standing in her front door. She pretended she hadn't seen her.

As he got in his car, she asked how his motel accommodations were.

He gave a non-definitive gesture with his hands and a smile of resignation. "Pretty good, as motels go," he said. "It's fairly clean and there's cable television, but . . ." He laughed. "I don't know. I'm afraid I'm rather paranoid about sleeping in a bed where so many other people have slept."

She laughed heartily and said she understood and felt exactly the same way. "Is it quiet enough?"

"No, it's not. The noise, in fact, is a real problem. It's right on the highway, as you know, and there seems to be no end of traffic." He slapped his hands against the steering wheel. "Oh well, maybe I'll get used to it."

She reached down to pull a weed from her marigold bed, something to give herself time to think about what she was about to say. "I'm so sorry about that. But you see, if you were a woman or if you'd brought your wife along, I could've put you up in one of my spare bedrooms. I've sometimes done that to save the judge some money." She looked embarrassed.

"That's very kind of you," he said. "But I don't have a wife. I'm divorced."

She played with the collar of her dress as her embarrassment flushed her face. "Oh goodness, I'm sorry, Mr. Riddick. That was so thoughtless of me to even mention such a thing."

He reached over and touched her hand gently. "That's perfectly all right. No need to apologize. It was an amicable agreement and we both seem to be adjusting nicely."

She didn't know what to say at this point. He smiled, thanked her for the hospitality, and said he must get back to his room.

That night, as she readied herself for bed, she began to feel embarrassed for having told Mr. Riddick so much about her childhood tragedy, especially so because she felt now that he probably hadn't wanted to know about it (after all, they were only strangers), and guilty because she realized that for a few minutes she had lost control of herself and had brought the long-suppressed experience forward. Because of that brief lapse, she now sensed the possible dangers of the imminent bad weather more keenly than she might have otherwise.

Before retiring, she walked to the living room, opened the front door and looked in all directions. Above and beyond the Massey house, she saw distant lightning, one rapid, silver burst after another, revealing the density and thoroughness of the cloud cover. She heard the overlapping tympani sounds of thunder which followed in unremitting sequence each thrust of lightning. Suddenly it all seemed so familiar, the oppressive heat and humidity, the lightning and thunder, the sense of awe and helplessness in coming face to face with God's wrath.

She recalled the pictures she had seen the other day of the Oklahoma tornado. She wondered if there had been pictures of the one that killed her mother and father. If so, Aunt Clara had probably hidden them so she wouldn't have to relive the experience. She tried, consciously now, to remember how it had been. It wasn't easy. It was a confused memory. She could recall only certain details. The rest she had reconstructed during the stunned weeks and months following the storm, unwittingly filling in the blank spots with what she thought had happened. Now, as she walked back to her bedroom, she could remember only that at some single, horrible moment she had jumped from her bed and crawled under it. Yet she was not found under the bed, but crouched down in the hallway with the house twisted and collapsed around her.

She lay down and pulled the sheet up to her chin without realizing she had done so. She gripped the sheet with both hands and asked God to help her forget and to let her sleep.

6

WHEN SHE ARRIVED AT THE CHURCH NEXT morning, Marsha Dinwiddie was already there, sitting in her car reading a TV magazine. Her students were playing this morning and she wanted to help Miss Etta get things set up.

There had been a lot of heavy rain, thunder, and lightning during the night. The sky was congested. Mouse-colored clouds, dense and impatient, moved to the east. They changed shapes, merged one with another or disintegrated, sometimes letting the sun shine through. A thick, low cover of steam rose above the black-topped surface of the parking lot.

Miss Etta was feeling good and told Marsha all about driving Mr. Riddick around Montcrief yesterday afternoon. Marsha had an assortment of cookies and two big bottles of Coke for her students. Mr. Riddick was punctual. He looked rested and very handsome in a navy jacket and grey trousers. He greeted them graciously and Miss Etta introduced him to Mrs. Dinwiddie. As soon as he had set up his materials in the choir room, he visited with them. Two of Marsha's students arrived at the same time, and things got underway. As soon as Miss Etta saw that everything was going to be all right, she started to leave and told Marsha she'd come back before twelve.

"By the way," she said as she started out the door, "do you think we oughta take Mr. Riddick to lunch?"

"I'd wondered about that," Marsha said. "But let's not make it anything fancy. I think we really should."

Miss Etta pondered a moment. "Do you think he might like catfish?"

"I don't know, but there's one way of findin' out. I tell you what. I'll ask him when he takes his break and then let you know. I'll call you at home."

She beamed. "That's an excellent idea, Marsha! I know I can depend on you."

The catfish lunch turned out to be enjoyable. Mr. Riddick seemed more relaxed than he'd been the day before. When they returned to the church, they found Alice Mae Ingram and her twenty students. They had come over from Ashley, about twelve miles east of Montcrief. Alice Mae was clearly displeased that she and her students had been kept waiting. Most of her students were clustered around the piano, trying it out or waiting to do so. The others were running up and down the hall or back and forth to the bathroom.

Alice Mae was sixty-two and had never married. She was often heard to remark that she was luckier than most women. She always had as many children as she wanted and never had to marry any old man to get them. Today she was colorfully dressed with an orchid on one lapel of her white blazer and a chain around her neck with a rhinestone-studded treble clef sign hanging from it. She wore her glasses only if she absolutely had to. This being the case, her lipstick was usually applied by guess-work and her lips often looked lopsided or bigger or smaller than they actually were.

She was a conscientious teacher whose sole aim, as she often said, was to earn more superior scores than any other teacher. Most of her teaching was done in group lessons, which meant that Mr. Riddick was going to hear the same pieces many times today. She was fanatic about details and knew all kinds of entertaining ways to get her pupils to do things exactly right. Because she lived alone, she often had her students over for extra lessons, theory classes, parlor recitals, and little get-together parties of all kinds. She had devoted almost forty years of her life to making students over in her own image. She lived in and for every one of them and would stop at nothing to see that they got everything they deserved and, sometimes, even more.

Miss Etta apologized to Alice Mae for being late and told her Mr. Riddick would ring his bell when he was ready to begin.

"How can he begin when he doesn't even have my cards?" Alice Mae asked unpleasantly. "I'll take 'em to 'im."

Mr. Riddick had just come back from the bathroom and was laying out his materials when Alice Mae walked in. Since Miss Etta had failed to introduce her, she introduced herself. He smiled and said he was pleased to meet her.

She laid the cards on the table. They were filled out on her typewriter and were meticulously correct in every detail. As she laid them down, she lightly tapped around the sides of the stack to line them up precisely. Then she gently placed her left palm on them as though to bless them.

"I've brought you twenty of the finest students you're goin' to hear," she said and straightened, looking him right in the eye. "These are all hand-picked and skillfully nurtured students," she added. "You will find each of them to be superior."

He couldn't believe what he was hearing. It sounded almost as though she were giving him an order. He propped his hand under his chin and looked at her. This was going to be an ordeal requiring a great deal of control and diplomacy. He knew there were teachers like her but he'd never had to deal with one of them.

Alice Mae straightened the tilt of the orchid on her lapel, then stood erect with her hands folded in front of her.

Mr. Riddick gave a little laugh that signified nothing in particular. "I'm sure I'm in for a delightful afternoon," he said.

She shaped her lips into a crooked smile. He looked at the stack of cards, then at her. "I've got to confess, Miss Ingram, I've never had a teacher talk to me like this before. It makes me wonder why you've bothered to bring your students over if they are as fine as you say they are."

He could see she was trying to control her anger. She leaned over and looked directly into his eyes. "I'll tell you why I brought them over, Mr. Riddick." She had to stop and catch her breath. Her fierce eyes were stretched wide. "I brought my students over because I want them to get all the experience they can get. I tell them the audition is one of their rewards for achieving excellence. It strengthens their faith in themselves and in their teacher as well."

He opened two or three of the top cards while he tried to decide what to say next. He looked up again. No more smiles. "I see, Miss Ingram." Then he added more solemnly, "But I'm sure you realize that I'm the judge and it's my job and responsibility to determine how well your students play. That's what I'm going to do, but I assure you I will do it as fairly and as honestly as I know how. . . . Thank you, Miss Ingram. I'll be happy to talk with you later."

As she left she slammed the door.

Most teachers picked up their cards after all their students had played. Alice Mae, however, insisted on picking hers up whenever she felt like it. When her fifth student returned to the waiting room in tears, she decided it was time to see what was going on. Without waiting for Mr. Riddick to ring the bell, she walked into the choir room and said she wanted to see how her students were doing. His first impulse was to refuse to show her the cards but decided, instead, to let her have those he had already filled out. She opened each one and muttered to herself from time to time as she hastily read what he'd written and the scores he'd given. When she opened the last card and saw what he had given little Charlene Crosby, she was appalled. Mr. Riddick watched curiously.

She clamped her jaws together and her lop-sided lips quivered and almost disappeared. She leaned forward and laid the open card in front of him. "Now, Mr. Riddick, you didn't *really* mean this, did you?" She pointed to the words "very good." Her finger trembled.

He didn't need to look at the card. He could still hear what the musically inept little girl had just played. "But I do, Miss Ingram," he said firmly. "That little girl is virtually without musical talent."

She slapped the table top. "Mr. Riddick!" she shouted. "How can you sit there and say a thing like that? That child happens to be one of my best pupils, and the only reason she didn't play her best is because she was scared. She told me herself that you nearly scared her to death."

"It's entirely likely that I did scare her, Miss Ingram, but I certainly didn't intend to." He paused and ran his hands over the back of his head in an attempt to curb his temper. As he did so, he said, "Miss Ingram, I don't know what kind of person you think I am, but if you think I'm going to change that student's score, all I can say is that you have seriously misjudged me. . . . Now look, I'm never going to get through today at this rate. I'm afraid I'll have to ask you to leave now. Anything else you say will only make matters worse."

He didn't ring the bell again until he'd adjusted to what had just happened. He knew it was going to be difficult now to listen and think objectively, yet he was determined not to be negatively influenced by it. Ironically, his job was made easier since almost every one of Alice Mae's students played exceptionally well. His comments were usually about the sameness of the programs and the students' lack of personal and musical involvement in what they were playing. Almost without exception, every detail on the page was followed exactly, even though each performance sounded like the one before it, as though the student were simply imitating and carrying out instructions repeatedly given and rigorously enforced.

When Alice Mae picked up her cards, she asked if he had changed Charlene's score. When he smiled and said he had not, she drew the stack of cards to her body, her eyes narrowing and her jaws clamped so tightly that her neck muscles popped out. The orchid fell to the floor. She leaned over the desk and glared her anger into his eyes.

"I want to advise you, James Riddick, the Guild's goin' to hear from me about this! Don't think for a minute you're goin' to get away with it. And I can assure you that your so-called judgin' days are over!" She straightened quickly and threw her chin forward and down to emphasize her determination.

He leaned back and smiled. "Your orchid fell off, Miss Ingram," he said politely.

She gave a grunt and bent over to pick it up. The cards fell to the floor. She frantically gathered them up, picked up the orchid, and turned her back disdainfully on him.

"Thank you, Miss Ingram. I'm sorry about our differences but, in spite of that, in many ways I find your teaching commendable. Good luck!" She struggled the door open with an audible sigh of frustration and slammed it behind her.

When Mr. Riddick walked into the waiting room later, Miss Etta was convinced something unpleasant had happened. Just a few minutes earlier, Alice Mae had rushed into the waiting room, noisily gathered up her things, pulled little Charlene protectively to her side, and hurried out the door without acknowledging Miss Etta's presence or her proffered attempt at conversation.

Miss Etta was busily trying to put the waiting room in order when Mr. Riddick came in. "All finished?" she asked as she emptied the wastebasket. When she finished, she fidgeted with her hair, then wiped her handkerchief across her palms. "There!" she said. "Things are almost back to normal."

When he didn't reply immediately she felt a moment's discomfort. Finally, he said he was very tired and needed to get back to his room. He thanked her for lunch and said goodbye. She watched as he started to the door, stopped momentarily, and then left. She was disappointed. She had hoped he might like to go to her house again or ride around some more.

As she checked the choir room to see that everything was as it should be, and as she locked the church door, her feelings of uneasiness intensified. She was always so concerned that the auditions run smoothly. She hoped nothing serious had happened to upset Mr. Riddick. Oh dear, he's such a nice man, she thought as she walked to her car.

While she was driving home, she decided she would have Mr.

Riddick over for lunch tomorrow. She would call him from home to see if he would come. If so, she would plan her meal, run to the grocery store, and do some of the cooking tonight.

She got no answer the first time she called. When she phoned a little later and he answered, he said he'd had some more car trouble. The fellow who runs the City Garage had been kind enough to stop what he was doing and make some quick, minor adjustments. The car was running nicely now. The mechanic said he'd studied piano with her as a child and his youngest daughter was studying with her now, and they all evidently thought highly of her. He said he would be happy to have lunch with her but felt he was taking advantage of her hospitality. She laughed and assured him he wasn't.

Willie Belle Hawkins' students were scheduled to play all day Wednesday and Thursday morning. She called that night to ask Miss Etta how things were going so far. Miss Etta said she thought everything was going well.

Willie Belle gave a dry, sarcastic laugh. "Well, that's not what *I* heard."

Miss Etta laid down the knife she'd been using to cut up a cantaloupe. "I don't know what you mean, Willie Belle."

"I'm surprised you don't, Etta. Didn't Mr. Riddick say anything to you this afternoon after Alice Mae's students played?"

She thought for a moment. "Why no. But then he doesn't discuss the students he hears." Then she recalled the expression on his face when he came to the waiting room after hearing Alice Mae's students, and Alice Mae's peculiar behavior. "But you know, now that you mention it, he did look kinda' worried this afternoon. . . . But he didn't mention a thing to me." She felt herself getting weak. She knew something had happened.

". . . Etta, are you there?"

". . . Yes."

With renewed enthusiasm, "Well, Alice Mae called me about an hour ago and told me all about it. She said Mr. Riddick had scared little Charlene Crosby so bad she went to pieces and just messed up everything and that he graded her way down because of it. Then when Alice Mae went in to talk with him about it, he got real nasty and even asked her to leave the room. She said she was so upset she didn't know what to do. She said he thinks students should all be perfect and he won't make any allowances for anything. Furthermore, she said she's gonna write the Guild and demand that he not be allowed to judge anymore. . . . Etta, are you still there?"

She had sat down. She held her free hand over her heart. She didn't know if she could stand up. Yet in her distracted state she knew better than to give Willie Belle a chance to amplify the matter. "Willie Belle, I'm sure there's been some mistake. You saw him and had lunch with him. You saw what a fine man he is. And all the other teachers so far have been pleased."

"Well, I'm only tellin' you what Alice Mae told me, Etta. Now you know she's not makin' it all up."

Miss Etta cleared her throat a time or two and ran her hand across her brow. "No, I'm not sayin' that, Willie Belle. I just don't know what to think at this point. But in any case, that's a matter between Mr. Riddick and Alice Mae. I'm sure there's a satisfactory explanation for what happened."

"Well, anyway, I just wanted to let you know since you're in charge. You surely can understand why I'm concerned. After all, I've got forty-five kids playin' for him."

"Yes, Willie Belle, I do understand. . . . Thanks for callin'."

As she resumed the preparation of the fruit salad and later as she deboned the chicken for her casserole, she remembered Willie Belle's call with a stifling heaviness. Something about what Willie Belle had said troubled her. Most people who knew Alice Mae Ingram agreed she was just a typical old maid. All that boasting about having children without having a husband was sheer nonsense. And all that concern, that paranoia about winning superior scores, like other of her obsessions and quirks, only belied the real frustrated, unhappy woman underneath it all. Granted, her students played well but, like any other students, they often failed to do as well as she wanted them to. As for whether she would say anything to the Guild about the matter, Miss Etta had her doubts. And anyway, she thought, as she put the cover on the casserole and put it in the refrigerator, I'm not going to let it bother me. I have my own students to think about.

"That's mighty odd," Mabel Paradine said aloud to herself. She was referring to the fact that Miss Etta was home so early during audition week. Mabel had just finished watching her last soap opera and decided she'd go over and see what was up. She could take her nap later.

Miss Etta told her about having Mr. Riddick for lunch tomorrow. In spite of her efforts to put the conversation with Willie Belle out of her mind, she found it had left her more than slightly distressed. Mabel seemed to sense that something was wrong.

"How're the auditions goin'?" she asked as she leaned against the door facing.

Miss Etta told her about the call she'd just had from Willie Belle. "I'd just like for everything to run smoothly," she said. "Mr. Riddick seems like such a fine gentleman I'd hate for anything to spoil his visit with us."

Mabel knew Willie Belle and didn't like her. "Not bein' a musician and all, I don't know what kind of piano teacher she is, but I sure to God know what kind of person she is and I've got me no use for her. And if I was you, Etta, I wouldn't pay no attention to anything that old heifer says."

That's easy enough for Mabel to say, Miss Etta was thinking. And even though she felt much the same way about Willie Belle, she didn't want to be petty.

"What're you havin' tomorrow for lunch?" Mabel asked and sat down.

Miss Etta seemed more cheerful as she told her. She even took the chicken casserole out of the refrigerator and showed it to her.

"By the way, Etta, have you heard the news lately?"

She hadn't. She'd been too busy.

"Then you don't know about the tornado that hit Pine Valley?"

"No!" She clasped her left hand over her mouth. "When was that?"

"This mornin'. Didn't you see all them dark clouds over in that direction about mid-mornin'?"

She had indeed seen them and she remembered how uneasy she felt.

Mabel told her what she'd just heard on a special news bulletin while she was watching "Guiding Light." The worst damage had occurred at a trailer park where three of the five trailers had been destroyed. She spared none of the dreadful details. She was so excited about the news and so eager to pass it on that she failed to realize what effect it would have on Miss Etta. When she told her about a ten-year-old girl who had literally been vacuumed up by the wind and impaled on a tree limb, she could see she'd been too graphic. She knew about Miss Etta's childhood experience. She apologized and put her arms around Miss Etta. "I simply wuddn't thinkin'," she said.

After Mabel left, Miss Etta went to the front porch to see how things looked. Her concern now was more about the weather than about Willie Belle and Alice Mae. The part of the sky she could see suggested there was still more bad weather to come. Three different and clearly distinct cloud layers appeared to be in a state of arrested animation. The first and most distant layer was unbroken and dark grey. The second looked like photo stills of smokestack emissions leaning slightly to the north. Superimposed upon this was a much nearer accumulation of rotund white puffs of clouds piled high on top of one another like a million giant scoops of ice cream.

Across the street, Annie Pearl Massey drove into her driveway, got out of the car, and started inside the house. She saw Miss Etta and waved. Miss Etta waved back. Even after she put her hands together in front of her, she felt like waving again. Suddenly, deep down inside, she wished Annie Pearl would come over and talk a while. But Annie Pearl didn't. She went on inside the house and stopped only long enough to turn and latch the screen door.

Miss Etta had a look at her plants on the porch. She pulled a withered leaf from one and then another and lightly loosened the dirt around a pepper plant with her finger. Two or three times she straightened, rubbed her hands together to knock the dirt off, looked at the sky, then to Annie Pearl's house. She saw the newspaper lying near the ditch and went to get it. Reading it would give her something to do and maybe help her relax. That night, before going to sleep, she planned step by step how she would get everything done in the morning and how she would dress the dining room table for lunch.

Some of Willie Belle's students were waiting at the church next morning, and when Miss Etta let them in, they asked if they could practice on the piano. When she went to the kitchen to put on the coffee, she looked out and saw Mr. Riddick parking his car. She touched her fingers to her hair and smoothed down the front of her skirt. As she watched the steady dripping and spattering of the coffee, she heard him come in the back door. She turned as he came into the kitchen.

"Well," she said, clasping her hands to her chin. "And how did you sleep last night?"

"Better than the night before," he answered.

"Oh, I'm so glad to hear that," she said. "I'm sorry things aren't more comfortable at the motel."

"Don't worry. I'll manage." He looked at his watch as he heard the piano down the hall. "Is Mrs. Hawkins already here?"

"No, but some of her students are. They're tryin' out the piano. She'll probably be here in a few minutes." She reached into the cabinet and got a stack of paper cups. "How 'bout a cup of freshly brewed coffee?"

He sat down as she handed him the coffee. After he took one or two swallows, he smiled enigmatically and seemed about to say something when Willie Belle arrived. He had almost told Miss Etta that Jonell Sumrall had called him last night.

As Willie Belle laid the stack of cards on the table, she laughed. "Look at that, would you! I stayed up half the night fillin' those darned things out. And that's not even all of 'em. These are just the ones playin' today."

Miss Etta agreed that filling out the report cards was a problem. "Every year I find it harder and harder to do," she said.

Mr. Riddick abruptly put his cup down and laughed. "That reminds me," he said. "Speaking of those cards, I saw something yesterday I've never seen before in all the years I've been judging. Miss Ingram, that last lady yesterday, had filled out her cards on the typewriter." Then, with a sudden change of expression on his face, he looked out the window. "And you know, I completely forgot to compliment her for it."

Willie Belle and Miss Etta exchanged glances.

"Oh, Alice Mae Ingram always does things just right," Willie Belle said. "She's extremely conscientious about everything she does. And those students of hers are her very life."

"It didn't take long for me to realize that," he added.

Willie Belle looked at Miss Etta again. Miss Etta cleared her throat and asked if he would like to begin now. She was getting a little fidgety about the things she yet had to do.

As he got up to leave, Willie Belle handed him the cards. "Now, Mr. Riddick, I hope you're not expectin' to hear any concert pianists today. After all, you know these are only little kids, not college students. And some of 'em scare real easy."

He took the cards and thanked her with a smile. "I promise to be as kind and honest as possible." He turned to Miss Etta. "Oh, and I'll see you at noon, Mrs. Armstrong."

She nodded her head. "I'll come back and pick you up."

After he left, Willie Belle poured herself a cup of coffee. "Etta, are you takin' him to lunch again?"

"No, I'm havin' him over at my house for lunch." She picked up her purse and car keys. "You know," she said as she stopped at the door, "I'm very fond of that young man. I'm beginnin' to feel like he's the son I never had."

"That's sweet, Etta. But watch out now and don't let your motherly instincts get the best of you!"

She blushed. "Oh, my goodness, Willie Belle! You oughta be ashamed of yourself. You do have the wildest imagination."

Willie Belle went over and put her arm around her. "I was only kiddin', Etta. You know that."

"Yes. . . . Well, if you run into any kind of trouble, call me at home. I'll see you a little before twelve."

7

WILLIE BELLE HAD HER EAR TO THE CHOIR room door. When she saw Miss Etta come in, she tip-toed over to where she was.

"How's it goin', Willie Belle?"

Willie Belle motioned her into the waiting room. She reached down to straighten her stockings. "The kids've all been scared to death of him. They say he's the hardest judge they've ever had to play for."

Miss Etta put her purse down. "Have you seen any of your cards yet?"

"No. I'm almost scared to look at 'em. I'm gonna wait till he's through with this batch. The kids say he makes 'em play all their pieces, and when he asks for a scale, he always picks the very hardest ones."

Miss Etta didn't know what to say. She took her handkerchief and wiped her forehead, then dabbed it on her upper lip. "Well, it seems no two judges are alike, doesn't it? I remember some of my students sayin' last year that Mr. Scanlan was so kind he'd always ask for only the easy scales."

"Well, why does this fellow have to be so darned hard? I think it's because he's used to teachin' college students. And Etta, you know as well as I do it's not fair to grade these kids like college kids. After all, it's not a contest. It's supposed to be fun."

Miss Etta sat down and folded her hands on her knees. "Well, I just don't know," she said and wiped her upper lip again.

Willie Belle walked out and said she was going to listen to the rest of Frieda Hemphill's audition. In a few minutes, she and Frieda returned. Willie Belle straightened the ribbon around Frieda's pony-tail. "Tell us about your audition, honey. What did Mr. Riddick say to you? Was he very hard? And did he scare you?"

Frieda flapped her music against her legs. Whatever had transpired in the choir room, it didn't seem to have affected her negatively. "No'm, I wuttn't really scared. He was strict, though."

"Did he make you nervous to where you couldn't play your pieces?" Willie Belle asked and turned to look at Miss Etta.

"No'm. I couldn't get through the Bach and the Clementi 'cause I hattn't memorized 'em yet. But you told me it dittn't matter if I dittn't play all my pieces for memory 'cause he wuttn't s'posed to hear 'em all anyway."

Willie Belle straightened stiffly and made several emphatic nods with her head.

"You hear that, Etta? Now you see what I'm talkin' about. Don't you think he's bein' unreasonable?"

Miss Etta made a nervous sound in her throat. "Well, not exactly, Willie Belle. The syllabus specifically states that unless the program is long, the judge will hear all the pieces."

"Well, I don't remember ever seein' that in there. I just think it's perfectly ridiculous." She walked nervously around the room, frowning and stopping every now and then to straighten her stockings. About that time, Mr. Riddick came into the room with his briefcase and her report cards. Willie Belle took the cards and put them next to her purse on the table. She turned to Frieda.

"Is mother gonna pick you up, honey, or do you want me to take you home?" She seemed eager to get out of the church.

Frieda kept flapping her music against her legs. "Mother said she was gonna pick me up."

Willie Belle picked up her purse and the cards. "Well, in that case I'm gonna run on home and get a bite to eat." Then to Miss

Etta and Mr. Riddick without looking at either of them, "I'll see y'all after a while."

After she said the blessing and they had started eating, Miss Etta sensed that Mr. Riddick wasn't as relaxed as she had hoped he would be. She made repeated attempts to get a conversation going, but he seemed only half interested in what she was saying.

"Are you feelin' all right, Mr. Riddick?" she asked, laying her fork down and folding her hands under her chin.

He apologized for being distracted and attempted a smile. "Sometimes I find it hard to recover from some of what I hear." He reached over and patted her hand. "But I'm sorry, Mrs. Armstrong. The food is very delicious and beautiful to look at as well. I'm sure you worked very hard getting it ready."

She could tell he was making a special effort to be nice. She moved the food around on her plate without ever taking a bite of it. She wondered if she should say what she'd been thinking since they left the church. Without taking the fork from her plate, she looked up. His eyes were intently on her face. She found it even harder to get the words out.

"I've often wondered if it's possible for judges to do their job without causin' hard feelin's." She took a small bite of the casserole. "Don't you find it frustratin', Mr. Riddick?"

He asked if he could have some more tea. As he stirred it, he asked, "Have I caused some hard feelings, Mrs. Armstrong?" Then he laughed. "I don't know why I ask. I cause hard feelings everywhere I go." He stopped eating, held the glass of tea with both hands and looked at it before taking another sip.

"Perhaps you're right," Miss Etta said. "It's better not to talk about such things. I asked only because I can see how conscientious you are. You have extremely high ideals, and I know you must agonize over a lot of what you have to listen to."

She got the dessert from the refrigerator and began to serve it. "I've been thinkin' a lot since you've been here about the judges we've had in the past. To tell the truth, I can't remember when we had a judge I thought was strict enough. They've all been so lenient, almost as though it was expected of 'em. I know many times my students have made higher scores than they deserved." She passed him the dessert and poured their coffee.

"Unfortunately, I think you're right. The thing I find most upsetting about judging is that so many teachers expect the judge to adjust his standards to suit their own particular students. As far as I'm concerned, there's only one standard and that's excellence. I don't care whether the students are taking piano for the fun of it or if they plan to major in it in college." He talked on and on. It was as though, by verbalizing his feelings about music to Miss Etta, he was purposely pulling his thoughts out of storage as a way of keeping himself on track or, in other words, lest he forget at a time when it was so urgent not to.

"Where is excellence?" he asked, not rhetorically, but directly of her. She lowered her head. "I was brought up to value excellence and to work hard at it," he continued. "I could sooner cut off my fingers than I could compromise what I think is right and good."

Again he reached over and gently touched her hand. "I apologize, Mrs. Armstrong. I've done exactly what I've vowed many times before never to do again. I didn't mean to preach a sermon." He smiled. "But you know what? I believe, if I hadn't let off steam, I would have ended up with a bad headache or indigestion or both. I hope I haven't upset you."

She laughed so heartily she had to cover her mouth with her napkin. "Oh, my goodness, no, Mr. Riddick. I love hearin' you talk like that."

He seemed especially to enjoy the dessert and coffee. As he finished, he smiled, reached over and took her plate. "That was mighty fine food, Mrs. Armstrong." He stood, gathered up all the dishes while she protested, and took them to the sink. He came back and sat down again.

"You know what I'd like very much right now?" he asked.

"No, I don't. What's that, Mr. Riddick?"

He laughed and undid his tie. "I'd like for you to tell me some more about yourself. I'd especially like to hear more about your childhood. What happened, for instance, after the tornado, and when did you first start playing the piano?" He watched her face change. "Would that upset you?"

She played with her napkin, folding and unfolding it. "I'm afraid you wouldn't find my childhood very interestin', Mr. Riddick. I'd much rather hear about yours."

"My childhood, by comparison to yours, was too dull to talk about. Most ordinary. . . . I really would like to hear more about what happened after you lost your parents. That is, unless you'd rather not talk about it."

She laid the napkin down and folded her hands under her chin. She told him about being adopted by Aunt Clara and about her cousins, and especially about Uncle Lester. At one point she stopped and laughed, covering her mouth with the napkin. She looked down at the table and fingered the tablecloth. "I used to play Casino with my cousins. Jimmie Dale was the oldest and couldn't ever seem to win a game, no matter how hard he tried. He'd cheat and lie and do everything in order to win, but somehow I'd always get the best of him." She stopped again and chuckled. "I don't really know why I was always so lucky. But anyway, it always made Jimmie Dale mad, and he'd scream and holler and throw things and say all kinds of mean, nasty things. Sometimes Aunt Clara would come in and give him a tongue-lashin' or a whippin'.

"One day while we were playin' Casino, a bad storm came up and I got scared. Remember, I told you about crawlin' under the bed whenever the weather was bad? Well, as soon as it started lightnin', I ran and got under my bed, and as I was runnin' out of the livin' room, Jimmie Dale jumped up and hollered as loud as he could, 'Now you see, little ol' tacky Fayette Ramsey! God's gonna get even with you! He's givin' you fair warnin'. One of these days one of them lightnin' bolts is gonna have your name on it!'" She chuckled. "That's just the way he used to talk and Aunt Clara was always fussin' at 'im because of it. Anyway, after that, every time we'd have bad weather and there'd be lightnin', Jimmie Dale would punch me in the back and say, 'This one's got your name on it, little cheat!'" She had grown solemn now and distracted.

She started to get up but didn't. She put both hands on the edge of the table and looked straight ahead. Now she talked softly, tapping her fingers on the table. "I could never completely forget that. I tried to."

"But surely you didn't believe what he said?"

Without looking directly at him, she put one hand over her mouth and took a deep breath. "I suppose I did. I never told anybody except Aunt Clara that I felt I was responsible for my parents' death."

"How could you possibly think that?"

She studied for a while. "At this very moment I really don't know. But at the time I seem to remember that I had failed to do somethin' I ought to have done." She turned to face him. "I really don't know what it was. I do remember, though, that whenever I talked to Aunt Clara about it, she always tried to console me and assure me there was nothin' I could have done to save my mother and daddy."

"Yet you continued to feel guilty?"

"Yes."

"Do you still feel guilty?"

She turned her head to one side and bit her bottom lip. She started to say something but stopped, then faced him and smiled. "That was long, long ago, Mr. Riddick. I'm not at all sure what I feel now."

Before they returned to the church, Virgiline Canfield called and wanted to know if Miss Etta and Mr. Riddick would have dinner with her at her home Thursday evening. Willie Belle would also be there. Mr. Riddick said the ladies were spoiling him but he was enjoying it.

That night, Willie Belle called again to tell her things had not gone well that afternoon. She repeated her claim that Mr. Riddick was unreasonable and unfit to judge children. She planned to have a long talk with him tomorrow after all of her students had played and set him straight about a few things. Miss Etta didn't comment because she knew Willie Belle didn't expect her to. Afterwards, she decided she didn't need to go to the church in the morning. In fact, she felt better once she'd made up her mind. She'd call Willie Belle and Mr. Riddick later and tell them she wouldn't be there.

When she went to the church about twelve-thirty next day, she found Mr. Thurman Beardsley and two of his students in the waiting room. She asked if they'd had lunch. They said they had.

"Would you like some coffee, Mr. Beardsley?" she asked, looking into the kitchen to see if there were any left.

"I would dearly love some," he said precisely, with an atypical southern accent. Ever since he went up north to study and people laughed at the way he talked, he had developed a manner of speaking in public which was as amusing down south as his normal manner of speaking had been up north. To set himself even farther apart from the local folks, he pronounced common, everyday words and names with broad "a's," and foreign words and names with dubious accuracy which some folks mistook for the real thing.

As he followed her into the kitchen, Miss Etta got a pungent whiff of his after-shave. "And what about your students? Would they like some Coke or some punch?"

"No, m'am," they both answered from the other room.

Miss Etta liked Mr. Beardsley in spite of the fact that some people, especially those meeting him for the first time, thought he was a bit odd. He was slight of stature, meticulous to a fault, and effeminate. Many people found it hard to reconcile what they saw and heard with the fact that he was married and the father of three children.

As a child in a small town where boys who studied piano were called sissies, he had become aware by the time he was ten of his disparity with other boys his own age. Instead of trying to be like them, he enjoyed being different and took pride in doing so. As he got older, his physical mannerisms became more pronounced. The questioning looks he often got in public, rather than embarrassing him, gave him almost as much satisfaction as his piano playing did.

Now, as he and Miss Etta talked, he took a dainty sip of coffee and fingered the rim of the cup. He asked her what kind of technical exercises she gave her students and, when she said she seldom used them, he seemed shocked. "I find technical exercises indispensable," he said. "I practice them religiously for an hour every morning. I simply could not play my repertoire otherwise."

Miss Etta had heard all of this many times before. Everyone knew he was fanatic about piano technique. When he used the word, which was often, he stressed the first syllable snappily. Sometimes some of the other teachers would imitate him and have a good laugh.

Miss Etta was not concentrating on what he was saying, though she gave the impression that she was. As she looked into her coffee cup, she smiled, not at what he was saying, but upon remembering a remark he had made several years ago following a performance of a Beethoven sonata by a local pianist. "One has to suffer in order to play Beethoven," he had said with supreme authority. Folks had laughed about that for weeks.

Mr. Riddick arrived, his suit coat thrown over his shoulder. When Miss Etta introduced the two men, Mr. Beardsley smiled broadly and squeezed Mr. Riddick's hand as though to confirm the pleasure he felt at meeting him. "I'm simply delighted, Mr. Riddick! I've heard so many fine things about you." His eyes were making a quick appraisal of Mr. Riddick's appearance. "I do hope we have some time to talk later. I'd love to hear your ideas on technique."

Miss Etta turned away from them and smiled into her handkerchief.

It was time to begin. Miss Etta told Mr. Beardsley there were some cookies in the kitchen in case he or his students wanted some. He would know how to manage his own pupils' auditions, so she would go home for a while.

A few minutes later, as she was going out her front door, the phone rang. It was Virgiline, calling about Willie Belle. She spoke softly, as though Willie Belle were standing close by. Willie Belle had called between twelve and one o'clock to tell her she wouldn't be coming to dinner tonight. She had then gone into an emotional account of Mr. Riddick's judging and Mr. Riddick himself. "She said we should all get together and write a letter to the Guild about him."

"And what do you think, Virgiline?"

"Frankly, I think she's bein' unreasonable. You know I told you, Etta, I'm more than pleased with my scores. And furthermore, for somebody who says she doesn't take the auditions as seriously as you do, she surely has got herself worked up over 'em."

"Yes, I agree. . . . Then let that be the end of it. I believe Willie Belle will get over it."

That night, before going to sleep, she became concerned for the first time about how her own students would play tomorrow. At no other time in the past had she been so apprehensive. She had learned long ago that fretting about your students at this stage was a waste of energy and, in a real sense, it was detrimental to the students themselves. They could sense such apprehension. When you felt you'd done everything you could, you could make life easier for yourself by sitting back and letting rather than trying to make things happen.

Yet, why was she more concerned now than before? She went down the list of her students, reassessing their capabilities and trying to predict how each would do and what score each would probably make. This made her even more nervous. It was shocking how few of them were adequately prepared. She questioned her own adequacy as a teacher. How well had she done her job? Certainly as well as she had done for the last ten years, perhaps. Maybe slightly less. Her pupils had usually done well. The judges had seemed satisfied. And they had been so kind and complimentary . . . and lenient. Oh yes, that was the difference!

Mr. Riddick would tell each of them exactly what he thought. This much she knew for sure after talking with him and hearing from other teachers what he had said about their students. Most of her students would be disappointed and in other ways upset by their scores. They would hold her responsible for their failings and, in many cases, they would be justified. In every instance she would ultimately have to shoulder the responsibility.

Suddenly it became clear to her why she was more anxious now than before. Mr. Riddick would know her worth, or lack of it, as a teacher, and this would inevitably affect the way he felt about her as a person. She hadn't tried to impress him. She felt their relationship so far had been amiable and this satisfied her. It would be nice if they could become friends. He was such a fine man! And he would make such a fine friend!

To lament her shortcomings was futile. She was wise enough to know that. She would talk with him about her needs as a teacher and would consider the auditions a valuable learning experience. She hoped he wouldn't let her students' performances and her failings as a teacher diminish his regard for her.

She must get some sleep! She got up and warmed some milk. As she drank it, she was able to think more objectively about her situation. The milk made her feel better. She went to sleep.

The sudden onset of wind frightened her fully awake. It came in recurring wild gusts and swells and sounds like the screams of suffering children. For some time previously, she had been dimly aware of some kind of subterranean stimulus that made her turn from side to side. It was something visual—random blue-white illuminations that pervaded the room and penetrated her closed eyelids. She sat up, reached for her glasses and put them on. The wind coming in the partially raised windows billowed the ruffled curtains and blew paper and letters from the desk onto the floor. She hurried to the windows, closed them, and looked out in the direction of Mabel's house.

She turned the switch on the lamp but there was no light. Without thinking, she turned on the radio. Silence. She turned it off. Then it became clear to her.

"The electricity's off!" she said aloud and clasped both hands over her face. "Oh, dear God! We must be havin' a tornado!"

Without realizing how dangerous it was to do so, she hurried back to the windows, thinking she might be able to see Mabel next door. But how could that be possible when everything was in darkness? She nervously fingered some loose hair back into place and paced from one side of the bed to the other. Then it suddenly occurred to her, something from years and years ago. "I must get dressed!" she told herself, and started to the closet. The frequent fleeting flashes of lightning cast an eerie blue color on everything and made her cringe as it enveloped her. She pulled a dress from the closet and fumbled to get herself into it. She made agonized sounds of fear and frustration when she wasn't able to get herself buttoned up. She felt the collar touching her neck and distractedly fingered it back into place. She turned around and groped for the bed. . . . Should she try to crawl under it? Could she?

Suddenly she realized that the noise had subsided. The wind had ceased. There were still sprays of lightning but the swells, gusts, and screams had stopped. She went back to the window. She raised one of the shades and tried to see out. It was raining now, straight down, hard, and steadily. This made her feel better. Rain was a purge that sapped a storm of its strength. She made her way to the bed and decided to stay dressed, just in case. She lay down and put her glasses on the bedside table. She propped both pillows under her head. She felt safer this way. She could see what was happening without having to sit or stand up. She fidgeted and fingered her disheveled hair, raised up with a grunt, just long enough to feel if her collar were in place.

Except for the occasional lightning, the unchanging sound of the rain might have lulled her back to sleep. When a particular bolt of lightning struck and bounced off of something just outside her windows and the dynamite sound of ensuing thunder made her cover her ears with the ends of the pillow, she remembered again what Jimmie Dale used to say. She folded her hands on her chest and pondered the terror bad weather had for her. Although Jimmie Dale's taunting had a lot to do with it, her real fear of lightning had begun earlier.

Just a while ago, when she pulled a dress from the closet and the lightning bounced around her, she had had a fleeting, vague awareness that she was doing something she'd done before. But when? If there had been another such incident in her life, she was unable now to remember it clearly.

She recalled her conversation with Mr. Riddick yesterday. When he asked her if she still felt guilty about her parents' death, she hadn't known what to say. As she had grown older, she had realized how futile and destructive it was to continue feeling guilty for something that had happened so long ago, something that was over and done with, unchangeable, final. At some point during her growing up, she had decided that feeling guilty about her parents' death, like other dark feelings and fears, must be suppressed if she were to survive. She had gathered them all together and filed them in the most inaccessible region of her brain. In big, bold letters she had labeled the folder, "DO NOT DISTURB."

Then what was happening? Why was she disturbing those sealed and stored secrets? Until she told Mr. Riddick about her parents' death and her fear of bad weather, she had seldom, almost never, mentioned it to anyone else. Strangely enough, she had actually wanted to talk to Mr. Riddick about it. And too, hadn't her fear of storms and tornadoes become so overwhelming that she was no longer able to bear it alone? And was there, perhaps, some real but as yet unfathomable connection between her persistent and growing fear of tornadoes and her long-suppressed fear that God was trying to tell her something? Was He trying to change her? If so, why? . . . Maybe Jimmie Dale was right after all. Maybe God *was* trying to punish her.

The lightning had ceased. From the far distant reaches of the world outside came the periodic rumble of low, lazy and spent thunder, like the muted next-door sounds of a dozen pairs of busy feet on a shallow wooden floor. As she listened to the steady, slow rain, the bedside lamp suddenly came on. Now there was electricity. As she reached over and turned it off, she felt much better.

8

SHE DROVE SLOWER THAN USUAL TO THE church next morning because she knew the saturated black-topped streets were slippery. Everything was sodden. Some of the smaller chinaberry and oak trees were bent out of shape and drooped under the extra weight of water, and the pine tree trunks had darkened almost to black. Broken limbs and bright green foliage and matted pine straw littered her way and made her nervous.

When she took her eyes off of the road long enough to look upward, she felt better. The part of the sky she could see was clear, and the extremely close and oversized sun, like a wide-screen movie face seen from a front row seat, was just about to clear the tops of the trees to her left.

The high humidity level should have told her that all was not what it seemed to be. What she couldn't see behind her and beyond the trees was a slow-moving line of dingy, humpbacked clouds linked together at their lowest points like a herd of trunk-to-tail elephants on parade. One could only guess as to whether these were left-over remnants from last night's storm or the advance contingent of yet another storm to come.

Perhaps the worst of the weather was over, she thought. She slowly relaxed her shoulders and the tight grip on the steering wheel and thought about this special day of auditions. Whatever distress preceded events of this kind, the events themselves always created a festive excitement for her. Seeing all of her students dressed up in their best finery, dismissed from school for the occasion, and hearing them tell one another how scared they were and how glad they'd be when it was all over turned the event into a celebration. Every emotion was intensified. Today, students who normally did not associate with one another found unexpected pleasure in being together. The common bond was fear.

She indeed felt like a mother hen taking her brood to the circus. She couldn't possibly sense the dread so many of them felt. It had been too long since she last performed in public and, even so, she had never been afraid to play for others because she enjoyed and loved it so much.

The punch sloshed around and almost turned over as she hit a pothole just as she was turning into the parking lot. She quickly reached out with her right hand to keep a tray of cookies from sliding onto the floor. She had been thinking of other things. She knew the pothole was there; it had been there for years.

Once inside, she laid out the cookies, put the punch in the refrigerator, and made the coffee. After she had straightened the chairs in the waiting room and emptied the wastebasket, she checked on things in the choir room. She had just poured herself a cup of coffee when Mary Beth Simmons and her mother arrived.

"Good mornin', Lucille. And a special good mornin' to you, Mary Beth. How you feelin' this mornin'? All excited about your audition?"

Mary Beth leaned against the door facing. Holding her music behind her with both hands, she swung her body back and forth against the facing. She obviously did not feel like talking.

Lucille motioned Miss Etta into the kitchen. "I think she's real nervous, Miss Etta. She practiced a lot last night and again this mornin'. I knew she must be worried."

"Well, I'm sure everything'll go all right. . . . Now then, how 'bout some fresh coffee, Lucille?"

Lucille stirred a spoonful of artificial sweetener into her coffee and sat down on the front edge of the chair. "Wasn't that awful about the tornado last night?" she said.

Miss Etta took the cup from her mouth and held it with both hands. "What tornado, Lucille? You mean there's been another one?"

"Miss Etta, you mean you don't know about it?"

She put the cup down and stood up, walked to the sink for no good reason, then ran some water over her hands and dried them slowly and thoughtlessly. "I didn't turn my radio on this mornin'. I was runnin' late." She fingered the collar of her dress. "Is that why we had all that wind and rain last night?"

Lucille swallowed and nodded. "We were lucky that's all we had. Honey, that thing hit down not more'n ten miles from here. In the Rushton Community. You know where that is."

"Yes. Yes, of course. . . . Oh, my goodness!" Her fears returned full-force. She turned to the sink again and looked out the window, gripping the edge of the sink with both hands. She started to sit down, then got up again. She adjusted her glasses over her ears, lifted the cup of coffee to her mouth, then put it down without drinking any of it. "Well, then maybe the worst is over." She went over and looked out the window. "It surely looks like it. There're just a few clouds . . . little biddy ones . . . over yonder," she added, pointing to the northeast.

The fear in Miss Etta's voice was evident. As soon as Lucille finished her coffee, she rinsed out the cup and had a quick look out the window. "I sure do hope so. However, accordin' to the weather report I heard a while ago, there's more bad weather on the way."

Miss Etta made little nervous sounds in her throat as she distractedly rearranged the cookies on each of the trays and moved the trays from one part of the counter to another. With her back to Lucille, she closed her eyes, squeezed her hands together, and said a quick, impassioned prayer. She must have faith!

Mary Beth came to the kitchen door and leaned against it. She frowned and waved her music back and forth. "Mamma, I gotta go to the bathroom."

Lucille's glance at Miss Etta seemed to confirm what she'd just said about somebody's being nervous. "Well, run on, honey. You know where it is."

Miss Etta laid a hand on Mary Beth's head and leaned down and smiled at her. "You've got plenty of time, dear. Mr. Riddick hasn't come yet."

As soon as Mary Beth left, Mr. Riddick arrived. After Miss Etta introduced him to Lucille, he said today was going to be a special day. He was going to get to hear Mrs. Armstrong's students at long last. She felt a sudden weakness somewhere in the vicinity of her heart. This afternoon he would be finished. He would go home. She took a sip of coffee and gave a little weak smile. He excused himself and said it would take just a minute or two to get set up.

The ringing of the bell meant it was time for Mary Beth's audition. Miss Etta went with her and, as she opened the choir room door, introduced her to Mr. Riddick. Miss Etta left and Mary Beth stood alone, clutching her music. She was so nervous she didn't hear when he asked her for her music. The second time he asked, she heard. She walked apprehensively over to the desk, laid the music down and, frowning fiercely, stood looking at him.

He looked up, opened her report card, signed it, and told her she could go to the piano and start with whatever piece she preferred. She managed to position herself on the piano bench and her little freckled hands on the keys with a deep sigh of relief that he hadn't asked her to play a scale first. She made a fumbled attempt to begin "Jukebox Jamboree," but Mr. Riddick stopped her.

"Mary Beth, can you tell me what key 'Jukebox Jamboree' is in?"

She scowled. Should she say she didn't know or pretend she did? In either case, she knew she was already in trouble. Without looking at him or taking her hands from the keys, she nodded that she did.

"Very well," he said kindly, "let's play the scale and the cadences in that key, and then the piece. Is that all right?"

Mary Beth knew for sure that the whole thing was going to be a disaster. She found it hard to keep her hands from shaking and had to try three times before she could make both hands start on the same scale notes. She bit her lips, clamped her jaws together, squeezed down with all her might on her wrists, and never really knew what happened after that.

When the audition was over, Mr. Riddick thanked her. She didn't know whether to laugh or cry as she hurried back to the waiting room. Miss Etta met her in the hall and gave her a bright smile and a touch on her head which she didn't appreciate.

"How'd it go, Mary Beth?" Miss Etta asked, as if she didn't already know.

Mary Beth was shrewd enough to know nothing could be gained by telling the truth. She felt she'd been duped from the outset and she didn't intend for a moment to take any of the blame.

She threw her music on the floor and jumped on it. "I hate it! I hate it! And I ain't never go'n' play ag'in!"

Miss Etta tried to pull the little girl to her but was unable to. Mary Beth was not to be consoled. Miss Etta told her to pick up her music and come with her into the waiting room for some refreshments. There were several other students now awaiting their turns.

Miss Etta bent over and looked Mary Beth straight in the eye. "Now listen here, Mary Beth! That's enough of that! You get yourself calmed down and tell me everything that happened. . . . Right this minute!"

Mary Beth threw her music on the table. "He's the meanest judge I ever saw! He made me play ever' single one of my pieces and them old stupid scales too!"

"I told you, Mary Beth, that you'd have to play all your pieces and your scales. Now didn't I? Remember? Now you knew that before you went in there."

She stomped her feet repeatedly. "You did not! You did not! You said I could play whatever I wanted to."

Miss Etta clasped her hands tightly together and went into the kitchen.

Lucille Simmons took Mary Beth's shoulders in her hands and seemed unsure about whether to shake her or put her arms around her. She leaned down and wiped the disheveled hair from Mary Beth's face. "Now honey, you mustn't be rude to Miss Etta. You know she told you you'd have to play all your pieces. I remember hearin' her tell you."

"That ain't so! And I don't care what you or nobody else says, I ain't takin' no more ol' piano lessons! Never, never!"

Mary Beth crossed her arms on the table and pressed her chin as hard as she could against them. "Here, Mary Beth," Miss Etta said, putting some cookies and a glass of punch on the table, "eat some of Miss Etta's cookies and you'll feel a lot better."

When Mark and Monica Mayfield arrived an hour later, Mark was carrying a dead bird he'd found in the ditch and was trying to touch his sister with it.

Miss Etta hurried from the kitchen, alarmed by the commotion. "Monica! Mark! What on earth are y'all doin'? . . . Now y'all stop that this very minute! D'you hear me?"

Monica ran and stood behind her. "Look, Miss Etta! Mark's got a stinkin' old dead bird and he's tryin' to put it on me. Make him stop! Make him go throw that nasty old thing away."

Miss Etta grabbed Mark and pushed him toward the door. "Mark Mayfield, that's down-right disgustin'! How could you do a thing like that? You oughta be ashamed of yourself. Now, you go throw that poor old bird away right this minute and then you go straight to the bathroom and scour those hands of yours real good."

He doubled up with laughter. He laid his music down and ran outside, swinging the bird over his head.

While Mark was playing his audition, Miss Etta and Monica sat in the kitchen and had a nice little visit. Miss Etta drank coffee and Monica nibbled disinterestedly on a molasses cookie.

"Tell me all about the trip to Little Rock, Monica," Miss Etta said. "Was it fun? And did you find you a pretty recital dress?"

Monica's face brightened. "Oh yes, m'am! We had a very good time. But the very best part of all was buyin' my recital dress. I'm sure it's the prettiest dress I ever had. It's a pale blue and has some dark blue ribbons around the collar and the sleeves. Mother said it just needs a little takin' up in the waist and it'll fit perfectly. I'm so anxious for you to see it, Miss Etta."

Miss Etta was only half listening. She was remembering last Friday night and the despair she had suffered. Realizing suddenly that she wasn't paying attention, she smiled and reached over to touch Monica's hand. "I'm so glad you found just what you wanted, dear. Just think, one week from tomorrow's the recital and you'll get to wear it."

Monica finished her cookie and wiped her hands daintily on a napkin. Then, suddenly, her mood seemed to sadden. She studied Miss Etta's face from time to time without looking directly at her.

Miss Etta reached over and touched Monica's cheek. "Why the sad look all of a sudden, dear?" she asked.

Monica lined up the edges of her music and waited a while before answering. "Miss Etta," she said, almost in a whisper, "do you ever get lonesome?"

Miss Etta gave a little laugh. "Why, for goodness sakes, Monica! What ever makes you ask a thing like that?" She pulled her chin in and tried to look composed.

"I don't know exactly, but sometimes I think about you bein' all by yourself and how I'd feel if I didn't have anybody to live with. I don't believe I could stand it."

Miss Etta got up and moved about the kitchen, straightening this and that, trying to look busy doing nothing in particular. She stopped wiping the sink and, without turning, said, "Well now, you see, you're a little girl and you need to be with somebody all the time. But you must remember that Miss Etta has lots of responsibilities and lots of things to keep her busy. Why, I'm almost always doin' somethin'."

She turned and laid a gentle hand on Monica's shoulder. "But I appreciate your thoughtfulness and concern for me, dear. But you can see, for instance, how busy I am with the auditions. And remember, I've got the recital to worry about. And that's only part of it."

Monica got up suddenly and put her arms around Miss Etta's waist. She seemed about to cry. "I think you're such a sweet lady, Miss Etta. We all love you so much." She sniffed and wiped her nose with her napkin. "The other day on the way to Little Rock, Mother was sayin' how she wished you'd gone with us. She said she was afraid you might be lonesome all by yourself."

She couldn't answer. She took several deep breaths and tried to control the muscles of her face and the tightening in her throat. She bent down and pulled Monica tightly to her. "Oh, oh, oh," she sighed.

Later, while Monica was playing her audition, Miss Etta walked to the outside door and looked out while Mark entertained himself by kicking rocks up and down the street. She couldn't help thinking about what Monica had said. In the short space of a minute, she had been stripped and exposed, the dubious comfort of her involvement in the auditions diluted by old thoughts and concerns. It was not Monica's fault.

For the last day or so, she had been forced to look beyond the auditions. She tried valiantly to exult in the moment, to nurture it and be shielded by it, but more and more she realized to what extent her thoughts now projected beyond the happy present instead of savoring it for all it was worth. Soon, in a matter of a few hours, the auditions would be over. Mr. Riddick would be gone. The weekend, like all the coming days of her life, promised nothing but desolation, and her will to cope with it was growing weaker by the hour. One distressful thought led to another, and soon she was thinking about Annette. In turn, when she thought of Annette, she thought of Bob and her guilt returned perceptibly. She hadn't written the letter to Annette last weekend as she'd planned to do. She must surely do so soon. But how could she write without mentioning Bob, and what could she say about Bob without being dishonest?

Three more of her students arrived. They giggled when they saw her and made exaggerated gestures to show how nervous they were.

Lanelle Morgan, the church secretary, came tip-toeing down the hall and told her there was a phone call for her in the office.

"Who is it, Lanelle? Do you know?"

"It's Jonell Sumrall, Miss Etta. She says it's very important."

She clasped her hands together as they hurried to the office. "Oh dear! I wonder what's happened." She trembled as she picked up the phone. "Hello, Jonell. This is Miss Etta. What's the matter? Has somethin' happened?"

"Oh, hi, Miss Etta." She laughed hoarsely. "Look, I'm really sorry to bother you this way, but somethin's come up and I was wonderin' if I could possibly change places with Mollie Hong this afternoon. I'm just not gonna be able to make it by two-thirty."

"Why, Jonell, that wouldn't be right. Mollie's countin' on comin' at four. She's the very last one to play."

"But I've already talked with her, Miss Etta, and she said she'd change places with me if you said it was okay. I promise you that's what she said. She said she could come at two-thirty just as easy as at four. . . . Please say it's all right. I promise I'll explain everything later. Okay?"

She deliberated. She didn't like to change things. "Oh dear, that means I'll have to tell Mr. Riddick about the change and rearrange the cards for him. . . . Oh, mercy me! . . . Jonell, dear, are you sure Mollie said it would be all right?"

Jonell dabbed her cigarette out and gave another husky laugh. "I promise you, as sure as God made little green apples, she said it was all right."

Miss Etta still hesitated. "Well," she said finally, "I suppose it'll work out all right. I'll mention it to Mr. Riddick at lunch."

"Oh, thanks a million, Miss Etta. You're a doll!"

The thing that displeased her most about making the change was that she had wanted her best student to play last. . . . Oh dear! What a difference between Jonell and Mollie!

She took Mr. Riddick to Sally's Country Diner for lunch. It was the most popular eating place in Montcrief, situated on a corner of Main Street. It was now a few minutes past twelve and the place was crowded and noisy. A thick, heavy smell of fried food and cigarette smoke lay like a cloying morning fog, suspended midway between the ceiling and the tops of people's heads and clearly defined by the unshielded reflected rays of the sun.

The tables were covered with red checkered oilcloths, and the salt and pepper shakers and the sugar and artificial sweetener bowls were made of crockery in the shapes of butter churns and molds. Ketchup and mustard were in yellow plastic dispensers shaped like ears of corn. On each table there was a vase of artificial flowers, the original exaggeratedly bright colors now dulled by dust and sun. The waitresses wore long skirts, aprons, and granny bonnets.

"Why hello, Miss Etta!" It was Doreen Staples, one of her former students now waiting tables. "I'm gonna have a table for you in just a minute. I've got some folks just fixin' to leave."

Miss Etta smiled and thanked her but couldn't remember her name. When they were seated and Doreen came to take their orders, Miss Etta thought she should introduce her to Mr. Riddick. When she confessed she couldn't remember her name, Doreen laughed and said she could understand why.

"I'm Doreen Staples, remember?" Then to Mr. Riddick, "Poor Miss Etta, bless her heart, she tried everything she could to teach me how to play the piano but I was too dumb to learn. I just wuddn't cut out for it."

Doreen, like most of the other waitresses, was miscast in her old fashioned clothes. Her eyes were heavily made up with eye shadow and mascara, and her thin lips were painted a lustrous red. While she waited for them to decide what they wanted, she preened the cuticles of one hand with the long, red nails of the other.

"Wha'chall go'n' have, Miss Etta?" She got off duty at one o'clock and was tired on her feet.

After they made their selections, Doreen asked, "Is this all one check?"

"Yes, Doreen, and I'm payin'," Miss Etta replied.

While they were waiting for their food, Leona Boxberger and Ina Mae Jones finished their meals and came over.

"Well, my goodness!" Miss Etta exclaimed. "I didn't see y'all over there. Mr. Riddick, I'd like you to meet some friends of mine.

Mrs. Boxberger and Mrs. Jones are retired school teachers. This is Mr. Riddick, our Guild judge from Louisiana."

Anyone could see they were happy to meet him. They talked with distressed faces about the tornado that hit the Rushton Community. Then Leona laughed quietly as though afraid she'd be heard. She clutched her purse to her waist. "All the young girls are talkin' about how good-lookin' you are, Mr. Riddick." And to Miss Etta, "I can see why, can't you?"

Miss Etta blushed and covered her mouth with her napkin. Mr. Riddick thanked her for the compliment and said he believed the students he'd heard so far had been too nervous to pay much attention to what he looked like.

"I huhd one guhl, who shall remain anonymous, say you looked for the wuhld like Robuht Redfuhd," Ina Mae said.

This amused the ladies and embarrassed Mr. Riddick. Doreen came with their meals and Leona and Ina Mae said goodbye and it had been a pleasure to meet Mr. Riddick. After Leona paid the cashier, she hurried back to the table where Miss Etta and Mr. Riddick were sitting.

"Oh Fayetta," she said, "I meant to ask you. When's your recital? I haven't seen a thing about it in the *Herald*."

She told her it was a week from tomorrow night.

"Well, I certainly plan to be there." She turned to Mr. Riddick. "Fayetta's recitals are always so wonderful! I haven't missed one in years."

Leona's remarks embarrassed her and made her uneasy. As she picked at her food, she wondered if she should bring up her students' performances. Leona's remarks left her little choice, she decided.

She cleared her throat. "Leona's not a musician, so you can't believe everything she says about me. As a matter of fact, I must confess I've been awfully concerned lately about my teachin' and I'm very eager to know what you think about the students you've heard so far." She stopped and wiped her mouth, then placed a hand on either side of her plate. "Or is this a fair question to ask at this time, Mr. Riddick?"

Her question did not seem to surprise him. Her nervousness was apparent. He laughed, laid his fork down and looked her straight in the eye. "Do you want the good things first or the bad ones?" he asked teasingly.

She squirmed and managed a weak smile. "You mean there are some good ones?"

He became serious. "Yes, of course there are. For one thing, you've got some talented students. Furthermore, most of those I've heard so far seem relaxed at the piano and seem to enjoy making music."

She was wondering how, if at all, she had been responsible for any of that. She listened attentively, neglecting her food entirely. From time to time she cleared her throat and picked at the tablecloth.

Most of what he told her she already knew. He mentioned specifically the need for better preparation generally—accuracy of notes, touch, dynamics, pedaling, memory, and scales. He told her he thought her students, as a whole, were above average rhythmically and that she should be happy about that because he considered rhythmic accuracy a matter of extreme importance. "I believe," he said finally, "that all children, until they reach a certain age and proficiency, should be more strictly disciplined than yours so far seem to be."

She was embarrassed and couldn't help showing it. No matter how broadly she tried to see things, she couldn't help equating her own obvious failings as a teacher with her failings as a person. Everything he said was so true! Not once did she attempt to fault her students for her own shortcomings. She thought she would cry outright if she didn't get a hold on herself. She pulled in her chin and smiled appreciatively.

He reached over, took her hands in his and gently squeezed them. "Have I been too unkind?"

She shook her head and stirred in her chair. "Oh, indeed not! You've been extremely kind and you'll never know how much it means to me." She moved her knife from one side of the plate to the other, then laid it down. "I don't know that I should mention this, but I've had a few phone calls about your judgin'. I hope this doesn't offend you. You're probably used to such things."

He nodded to indicate he was.

"I'm tellin' you this only because it has somethin' to do with what I'm goin' to say next." She waited a moment while she drank some tea. "I've always felt the judge has the right to grade students the way he wants to. I don't suppose I need tell you that not all teachers feel that way. I'm afraid they're more concerned about high scores than about good piano playin'. You see, Mr. Riddick . . . " Looking quickly around the room, she leaned slightly forward and lowered her voice. "Every judge we've had for the past ten years or so has been too lenient. We've all been able to get high scores when we really didn't deserve 'em. Do you know what I mean?"

He nodded. "I do indeed."

"What bothers me," she said after a slight hesitation, "is knowin' I've been guilty of lowerin' my own standards, even when I knew what I was doin'." She gave a little gasp and turned her eyes to the window. Then, as though talking to herself, she added, "I really don't think I have the courage or the respect to demand more from my students."

He reached over and patted her hand firmly. "Oh yes you do, Mrs. Armstrong! I know from what I've seen and heard of your students that you most certainly do have their respect. And as for your courage, there can be little doubt about that. Anyone who's gone through what you've gone through would need more than a little courage to do it. But in spite of that, I somehow suspect you've always had more than your share of it."

She looked surprised. "Why should you say a thing like that, Mr. Riddick?"

Again he laughed teasingly. "Aha! You see, some people have been telling *me* some things too. As a matter of fact, I know a lot more about you than only what you've told me. For instance, I know that you're a woman of great character and reputation. That's something I didn't have to be told, though. Furthermore, you're an anachronism. You're exceptional because you're honest." He touched her hand again. "And you know, Miss Etta, honesty is a rare commodity in our profession."

He called her Miss Etta! She felt her throat tightening again and her eyes beginning to burn. Oh dear! She simply mustn't cry. She turned her eyes to the window again and squeezed her hands together under the table.

He leaned across the table and tried to get her to look at him. She attempted a smile. He thumped the table. "Miss Etta, give me your attention!"

She turned around and burst into a happy laugh.

He grew serious once again. "I'd like to say something else, if I may, and hope it doesn't embarrass you." He paused, looked straight ahead as if, for an instant, he were somewhere else, then took a deep breath. "I know what a fine person you are. I've seen and felt it all this week. I didn't need anyone to tell me. You're full of love, for your students and for other human beings, and you're very kind and gentle. Your teaching reaches far beyond the walls of your living room." When he looked into the distance again, she wondered if he were going to say anything else.

He slowly turned and faced her. "In my lifetime I've had only three real teachers. That's a mighty small number, considering that I've had about thirty or more altogether. Those three teachers were all great musicians and great artists, but more important than that, they were great human beings." He stopped briefly to take a bite of the cobbler, then pushed it away. He wiped his mouth. "There's no way I could possibly tell you what it was they taught me. Certainly not just about music and how to play the piano. Something infinitely more valuable.

"I loved them all very much, but I loved Enrico Serti most of all." He hesitated, smiling. "There was one instance I'll never forget as long as I live. One day I went for a lesson without having prepared myself sufficiently because of some personal problems I was having at the time. I didn't play a single note at that lesson! Instead, he and I talked. At one point Dr. Serti laughed and said he thought sometimes he should have been a priest because he felt so deeply that his real purpose in life was to make people better. Teaching was secondary and only a way of accomplishing that mission."

She wanted to say something but couldn't. She withdrew her handkerchief from her purse and quickly covered her mouth. The gesture failed to avert a flood of tears.

"I didn't mean to upset you," he said softly.

She took off her glasses and wiped her eyes, then took a few deep breaths and shook her head several times. At last she was able to construct a wan smile. He smiled back and gently touched her hand.

"Now tell me, Miss Etta, how in the world do you hope to get through the rest of the day on what little you've eaten?" he teased.

She laughed as she opened her purse and took out her wallet. She got Doreen's attention and asked for the check. He asked if he might leave the tip. She said he could.

Outside, before getting into the car, she told him it was the best meal she'd had in ages!

In her happy state of mind, she failed to note, except slightly, how abruptly and drastically the weather had changed.

9

REBECCA BARNES AND JANE ELLEN SHOEmaker had already played their auditions and Tommy Thornhill was now playing his. Miss Etta had given him a handful of cookies and a big glass of punch to put him in the right frame of mind. She was in the kitchen, looking distractedly at the half-empty coffee carafe and wondering if she should make more coffee. She heard someone come in.

"Here I am, Miss Etta." It was Gamaliel Barrett, bright-eyed and smiling. Under one arm he held his music and under the other a large package.

Miss Etta swung around. When she saw who it was, she leaned forward and put her hands on her knees. "Well, hello, Gamaliel! Now don't you look handsome! And don't you look excited, too!" She cupped her hand under his chin and squeezed it gently. He beamed a big smile full of perfect white teeth. "Well, this is it, young man. The day you've been waitin' for. . . . But good gracious alive, Gamaliel! What on earth is that you've got there in that big ol' box?"

Seeing he was about to drop the box as he tried to lay his music on the table, Miss Etta offered to help him. He tightened his arm around the box but gave her his music. Then, beaming, he handed the box to her.

"Is this for me?" she asked, covering her mouth with her hands.

"Yessum, yessum! Go on! Open it!"

She was stunned. She put it on the table but was too nervous to open it. She covered her mouth again and muffled several more my goodnesses. She turned it over to see where to start.

"Why don'chu open it?" Gamaliel asked, wringing his hands.

"Oh dear," she said time and time again as she nervously unwrapped it. The paper was two brown grocery bags reversed and taped together. The box itself, bearing the logo of a local store, had been used before and was now sealed with Scotch tape. Unable to break the tape, she quickly drew a knife from the drawer and slit the box open. When she saw what was in it, she grew weak. Gamaliel's eyes were riveted on her face and his mouth agape as he waited to see what she would say.

She lifted from the box a white tablecloth with a border of hand-embroidered flowers of every color. With both arms extended as far as she could spread them, she held the tablecloth in front of her and stared in disbelief. Then, as she felt the tears filling her eyes, she gathered it together and held it tightly to her body. Gamaliel looked puzzled by her reaction.

She folded it and gently, carefully laid it back in the box, then stood looking into Gamaliel's eyes. She suddenly grabbed him, pulled him to her and squeezed him, saying his name over and over. When he put his arms around her neck, she broke into a spasm of tears.

Finally he said, "There's a note in the box too."

She wiped her eyes and looked for it. It had gotten mixed up with the wrapping paper. She bit her lips as she read it. The note had been written with a pencil and the writing was large and labored. "To Mrs. Armstrong with appreciation friendship and love. Philamena Barrett."

She put the note back in the envelope and pressed it to her heart. "How sweet! How sweet and how perfectly wonderful! Oh, Gamaliel, how can I ever tell you how much this means to me?" She bent over once more and hugged him and held him close.

Gamaliel was pleased. He played with a corner of the wrapping paper and shifted from one foot to the other as though trying more fully to comprehend Miss Etta's emotional reaction.

She stood in front of him with her hands folded, smiling. Finally she said, "Your mother's been workin' on this tablecloth for a long time, hasn't she?"

"Yessum." Then he suddenly laughed. "You near 'bout caught her last Friday. Remember when you came out to the car to talk to her? She knocked it over on the floor and was scared you might've done seen it."

"Well, for goodness sakes, that's right. Now that you mention it, I did notice her pickin' somethin' off the floor and crammin' it in her basket. . . . But tell me somethin', Gamaliel. How did your mother know how big to make it?"

He laughed again. "I'll show you," he said proudly, then walked from one end of the table to the other and on around, measuring it with his little hands spread as far as they would go. "One day while you were teachin' and I was waitin' in the kitchen, I snuck in your dinin' room and measured the table like Mamma told me to do."

She gave a hearty laugh and clapped her hands together. "Well, if that doesn't beat all I ever heard!" She bent down and pulled him to her again. "You're a regular little rascal, Gamaliel Barrett, d'you know that? . . . Now, where's your mother? Outside?"

"No'm, she went t'town. She said she'd be back directly."

"Good! I certainly want to see her and thank her personally for this wonderful surprise."

Knowing Mrs. Barrett would wait outside when she came to get Gamaliel, Miss Etta went to the back door to make sure she didn't miss her. In the meantime, Joan Switzer, Monita Brownlee, and Monita's mother Bernice arrived. Miss Etta stepped outside so they could talk without disturbing Mr. Riddick.

The girls were nervous and asked a lot of questions about the judge. Miss Etta assured them he was a fine man and a fine judge and that they had nothing to fear. Bernice Brownlee said she and the girls had just returned from seeing the tornado damage in the Rushton Community. Miss Etta was noticeably upset by the account and kept her handkerchief over her mouth as she listened reluctantly. At one point, Monita started to describe a particularly dreadful sight she'd seen when her mother nudged her and signaled with her eyes not to say anymore.

"Bernice, do you think we're gonna have a tornado?" Miss Etta asked.

"Well, I certainly hope not. Especially after seein' what we just saw. However, I hear we're still under a tornado watch."

Miss Etta cleared her throat. "We are? For how long?"

"Until four o'clock in the mornin'."

A sudden clap of thunder close by startled them. They hurried inside.

A few minutes afterwards, Gamaliel finished his audition and was so excited he couldn't stand still. Miss Etta poured him some punch and passed him a plate of cookies. In his excitement, he spilled the punch down the front of his shirt and dropped cookie crumbs on the floor. Miss Etta wiped his shirt with some paper towels and asked him all about his audition. He breathlessly told her every detail.

When the bell rang a few minutes later, Miss Etta gave Joan Switzer some words of advice and encouragement and sent her to the choir room. At about that time, Gamaliel decided to go outside to see if his mother were waiting. Miss Etta ran after him, making every effort to avoid disturbing Mr. Riddick. Mrs. Barrett hadn't come yet, so, with his hands in his pockets, Gamaliel walked out to the street and watched some children playing on the other side.

She called him back to where she was standing. "Now Gamaliel, I've got to get back inside, so I won't be able to stand out here and wait for your mother. But I want you to promise me you'll let me know the minute she comes, you hear?"

He promised he would.

She had just opened the door to go back inside when she heard someone call her name. Mollie Hong was just getting out of her father's car. Mr. Hong waved at her and smiled. Mollie ran to where Miss Etta was standing and put her arm around her waist.

"How are you, Miss Etta, and how are the auditions going?"

Mollie held the door open for her. "I'm just fine, Mollie dear. And I'd say things were goin' pretty well so far. But it'll all be over soon." There was a note of sadness in her voice.

"And I bet you'll be mighty glad, too."

She laughed. "Well, to be perfectly honest, I guess I will. . . . But how do you feel? You're not nervous, are you?"

Mollie threw her head back and laughed. "Yessum, I can't deny it. But I think I'm more excited than scared. Know what I mean?"

"Yes, sorta like on your weddin' day, as well as I remember."

They both had a good laugh.

When Monita Brownlee finished her audition, Miss Etta went to the choir room to remind Mr. Riddick it was time for his break. He said he preferred not to take a break and hoped he might finish a little early and be on his way home.

"Very well," she said matter-of-factly. She mustn't show her disappointment. "Then I'll send Mollie Hong on in. You remember I told you she and Jonell Sumrall swapped places."

He remembered. He had already opened Mollie's card and signed it.

Miss Etta was surprised to see Mrs. Barrett when she returned to the waiting room. She and Gamaliel were standing at the back of the room. Mrs. Barrett held both hands on the handle of her purse and listened with a pleased look in her eyes as Gamaliel talked to her.

"Mrs. Barrett!" Miss Etta exclaimed and clapped her hands together. "What a wonderful surprise! How delighted I am to see you!" She turned quickly to Mollie. "Oh, Mollie, I almost forgot. Mr. Riddick doesn't want to take a break, so you can go on and play now. . . . Are you ready, dear?"

Mollie was ready. She picked up her music from the table and went to the choir room, smiling and shaking her long, black hair loose from her shoulders.

"Good luck, dear."

Miss Etta hurried over to where Mrs. Barrett and Gamaliel stood. There was an awkward moment when neither of them knew what to do. Then Miss Etta moved closer and laid her hand on Mrs. Barrett's right arm. Mrs. Barrett released her right hand from the purse handle and allowed it to be held lightly and then squeezed. She smiled sadly and shifted her weight from one foot to the other. Softly she said, "Hello, Miz Armstrong."

"Oh, Mrs. Barrett, how can I ever tell you how much your beautiful gift means to me? It's one of the loveliest things anyone has ever done for me. I'm overwhelmed." Then, looking at Gamaliel, she added, "Gamaliel told me how he measured my dinin' room table so you'd know how big to make it. I do know that's one of the cleverest things I've ever heard of." She lowered her voice and clasped Mrs. Barrett's hand with both of hers. She patted it gently as tears filled her eyes. "I shall never forget this day."

"We're so glad you like it, Miz Armstrong. We jes wanted t'do a little sumpn fuh ya." She handed her purse to Gamaliel and laid her other hand on top of Miss Etta's.

Mollie Hong's audition lasted over thirty minutes. When she returned to the waiting room and Miss Etta asked her how the audition went, she said she had enjoyed it very much, that he had asked her to play all of her pieces and was very complimentary. She said, also, that she thought she had played better than ever before even though the piano wasn't so good. He made her feel comfortable and proud.

"I'm sure you played beautifully, Mollie. You always do. And I'm so glad he liked your playin'. . . . He's such a fine man!" She put her face closer to Mollie's and whispered, "I only wish you could've played last, the way I planned it so he'd have somethin' really beautiful to remember on his way home." She laughed and covered her mouth.

Mollie hugged her. "Thank you, Miss Etta. That makes me feel even better."

"Well, what's done is done," she said and took a deep breath. "Now you come on in here and let me give you somethin' to restore your energy."

Mollie followed her. "But I'm not tired, Miss Etta. In fact, I think I could go right back in there and play it all over again. Do you know what I mean?"

"Yes, I certainly do. That's because playin' is your very life. And that's the way it oughta be."

While Mollie waited for her father to come for her, she and Miss Etta enjoyed visiting and talking about new music for next year.

It was a quarter past four when Jonell Sumrall finally got to the church, all out of breath. Inside the waiting room she gave Miss Etta a quick hug and a kiss on the cheek and apologized for being late.

"Good heavens, Jonell!" Miss Etta could hardly believe what she was seeing. "Why in the world did you come dressed like that? You know you're supposed to dress properly when you perform so why didn't you put on somethin' more appropriate? And furthermore, why are you so late?"

Jonell threw her music on the table and stomped her feet. "Miss Etta, I'm so mad I could eat nails! Some idiot ran a stop sign at the corner of Main and Magnolia and almost hit me broadside. I still don't know how in this world I kept from being creamed and my Stingray totaled." She stopped and pulled her shirt out from her body. "Oh, this? . . . Well, Miss Etta, I dressed like this 'cause I wanted to be real comfortable when I play." She shook her long hair loose and gritted her teeth. "Oh, when I think about that crazy fool and how close I came to bein' killed! Just like that!" She snapped her fingers.

"Well, I'm sorry about that. Just thank the good Lord it wasn't any worse. But now, Jonell, you've got to hurry. Mr. Riddick was hopin' to get through early so he could go home."

Jonell stood in front of the door separating the kitchen from the waiting room and stole a quick look at herself in the glass. Her eyes were heavily made up with mascara and blue shadow and her lips were painted a translucent silver. Her long, brown hair was brushed straight down, covering her ears and taking a graceful, delicate turn inward under her cheeks. Over her strained designer jeans she wore one of her brother's long-sleeved shirts with the sleeves rolled up to her elbows and the top and bottom buttons open. The diverse emanations of "White Shoulders" and cigarette smoke fused into an incompatible, unpleasant odor. As she hurried to the choir room, she gave a husky cough and loosened another top button of her shirt.

As she entered, she fell back against the door, feigning exhaustion, gave a throaty laugh and said, "Hi there, I'm Jonell. Sorry to be late. This just hasn't been my day." She walked slowly over to the desk, holding her music close to her body and doing whatever else she could to make herself appealing.

Mr. Riddick turned down the page of the paperback novel he was reading and laid the book in his briefcase. As he signed her card, he looked up and smiled. "So, you finally made it. We'd begun to think you weren't coming."

"I almost didn't." She seemed encouraged that he had finally smiled and said something. "I just missed bein' clobbered on my way over here by some maniac." She laid her music down on top of the card, tossed her head to one side, and gave a hearty, husky laugh. "My Lord, it's true! If I didn't know better I'd swear you were Robert Redford. Some of my friends said you looked just like 'im but I said I'd believe it when I saw you."

"Are you trying to soft-soap me because you're late?"

She threw her head back and ran her fingers slowly, lazily through her hair in a gesture which, to Mr. Riddick, seemed to have been preconceived and carefully rehearsed as a way of making herself look sensuous and desirable. "No, I really mean it. The resemblance is uncanny!"

He put her music in order, opened the volume of Chopin Waltzes, and was trying to find the one she was going to play. She leaned down and showed him which one it was. Her face came close to his. Her hair, like her music, reeked of cigarette smoke.

He pulled her card from beneath the stack of music, opened it, looked up, and smiled. "What say we get started? What would you like to play first?"

She seemed not to have heard. Then suddenly, "Oh, okay." She went over and sat down at the piano, rubbing her hands together and laughing self-consciously. "Here's hopin'," she said, then ran a spastic C major scale to check out the piano. She grimaced and turned to him. "Good Lord! This piano's atrocious!" She brushed her hand lightly up and down the keyboard as though wiping dust from the keys. Then finally, "Okay, I guess I'm ready." She looked at him and waited.

"I asked what would you like to play first," he repeated.

"Oh, I'm sorry. I didn't hear you."

Just as he expected, she wanted to play "The Entertainer." She started before he could remind her she was supposed to play the scale and the cadences first.

He was surprised that she was talented but not surprised that she was technically inept and undisciplined. He could tell she had been allowed to play this way too long, either thinking it did not matter or not caring if it did or did not. Since she did not listen to herself, she did not know how bad her playing was. He felt it his duty to tell her. She played the Scott Joplin piece without memory slips, but he knew it was only because she liked it and could identify with it. The other pieces were a different matter.

He felt compelled to remind students like Jonell that they were not really fooling anybody by being able to play something they liked and felt safe with, if even this poorly. He asked her to play the Bach Invention.

She covered her face with her hands in a gesture of panic. She threw her head back and tried to laugh. "I knew it! I just knew as sure as God made little green apples you were gonna ask me to play that one."

His suspicions were verified. "After you play F major scale and cadences, please."

She started the scale too fast. She went just so far and couldn't continue because she wasn't sure of the fingering. He asked her to start over and she did, but this time, somewhere between the first note and the last one two octaves higher, her left hand got behind the right one. She put the pedal down and managed to fake her way back. He noted her deficiency by putting a check mark in the appropriate place on the card.

Before attempting the Bach Invention, she folded her hands in her lap and stared at the keyboard. She almost put her right hand on the keys but pulled back uncertainly. She then placed her left hand cautiously on the keys but suddenly withdrew it also. After an agonized moment or so, she tried quietly to start but was unable to.

"It's in the key of F major," Mr. Riddick said.

In a desperate effort to get her nerves under control, she laughed and struck an F major chord. "Oh yeah! I knew that." She started the Invention, nevertheless, in the key of C. Finally, in desperation, she stopped, jumped up and pushed her hair away from her face. "Look," she said emphatically, her voice shaking out of control, "I'm simply too shook up after that near-miss with that fool a while ago." She stomped both feet and slapped the top of the piano. "I can play that stupid piece," she said between clenched teeth. "I promise you I can play it perfectly!"

He held the music out for her to see. "Come and have a look, then try it one more time."

She walked over, took the music and looked at it. It did not help, nor would it have helped if she tried it ten more times. She had never been able to play it, even with the music in front of her, and she had never liked it. In fact, all Bach was a bore with a capital B. That kind of music did absolutely nothing for her.

When she saw it was useless to pursue the matter, and after she had tried again to blame the close call in her Stingray for her nervousness, he asked her to play the Chopin Waltz. Though somewhat better than the Bach, it did nothing to alter his opinion of her or the score he would give her. At least she felt a genuine though unrefined affinity for the sensuous melodies and sonorous harmonies of Chopin. She oversentimentalized it with exaggerated, naive rubato and phrasing. When she finished, she seemed pleased with herself. Instead of extolling her performance, he entered two or three check marks at the appropriate places and asked her for the next piece.

When Jonell finished her audition, she apologized for not having done better and once more used the accident she nearly had as an excuse. She walked over and stood in front of the desk. "What beautiful handwritin'!" she exclaimed as she bent over and tried to see what he was writing. As she got closer, her hair lightly brushed his face. He stopped writing, closed the card abruptly, and looked at her.

She laughed hoarsely and straightened. "I was only tryin' to see what you were sayin' about me. Aren't you gonna let me see it?"

He tapped the pen repeatedly against the desk, then stood up. "No, Jonell, I'm not. You may see it when Mrs. Armstrong lets you. That's the way it's done. You're supposed to leave now so I can finish filling out your card. I'm already late and would appreciate if you'd go now so I can finish and be on my way."

She pushed his briefcase over and sat on the corner of the desk, threw one leg over the other and placed her right hand on the desk close to the card. She tossed her head back in a seductive manner. "Are you disappointed, Mr. Riddick?" she asked in a childish voice.

"You seem to be a little confused about what my job is, Jonell. I'm here to judge your piano playing, nothing more." As he reached over to lay his pen down, he looked straight into her blue-shadowed eyes and said deliberately, "I am frankly not interested in anything else."

She picked his pen up and rolled it around between her hands, then touched her face with it and almost put it in her mouth. "Do you really have to go back to Louisiana today, Mr. Riddick?"

"I don't know why that should be of concern to you. My job is over as soon as I finish your card. How about leaving so I can do that?"

She slowly handed him the pen, managing to touch his hand as she did so. "I s'pose that was pretty presumptuous of me. I'm sorry, Mr. Riddick. I was just hopin' you might stay over and I'd get a chance to see you again. Tomorrow's Saturday, you know, and I don't have to go to school. I guess what I was really hopin' was that you might wanna take me out tonight."

He was not surprised. He actually felt pity rather than disgust for her, yet wondered how such a young girl could become so brazen in such a short lifetime. "Would it surprise you a great deal, Jonell, to know that I'm not interested in taking you out? Has it occurred to you how ridiculous that suggestion is? . . . Tell me, Jonell, just how old are you?"

"Seventeen. I'll be eighteen in August."

He leaned back and put one arm over the back of the chair. "Do you mean to tell me you don't feel embarrassed by what you're doing, what you're suggesting? Don't you have any boyfriends your own age? Surely you must."

She slapped her leg and threw her head back. "Oh hell!" she said, "boys my age are borin'. I mean borin' with a great big capital B. If you wanna know the truth, they absolutely turn me off," she said, gesturing her hands outward in opposite directions. She reached over to touch his arm but he moved. "I'm more mature than other girls my age and that's why I like older men. Like you."

"Well, that's unfortunate, Jonell, because I'm not attracted to you. I don't mean that as an insult, just as a reminder that you can stop trying."

She stood and moved closer, folding her arms and making suggestive movements with her glossy silver lips. She took the music when he handed it to her, laid it back on the desk, then reached over with her left hand and tried to touch his face. "It's such a handsome face!" she said.

He pushed her hand away. "Shall I call Mrs. Armstrong or will you leave on your own?"

"You mean you'd do somethin' like that?" She started to sit down on the desk again but, as she did so, she inadvertently moved his briefcase which, in turn, knocked the little brass bell onto the floor.

Miss Etta had long ago cleared the kitchen and the waiting room and was now pacing the floor, wondering why it was taking Jonell so long. It was after five o'clock and she had been in there almost an hour. What on earth could be keeping her? She had thought of everything, even the possibility that Jonell might . . . Oh dear! She couldn't allow herself to think such a thing! The playing had stopped long ago. The longer she waited, the more apprehensive she became.

Then she heard the bell. Not as before, but she heard it, nevertheless, and quickly put her folded hands to her chin and bit her lips. Now what on earth could that mean? Why would he ring the bell? The auditions were over. She walked into the hall and started for the choir room, then suddenly stopped, gasped, and covered her mouth with her hands. She heard Mr. Riddick talking but couldn't understand what he was saying. Then she heard Jonell say something which, if she heard correctly, astonished her. Yet she couldn't just stand there as though she were eavesdropping. She tried to steady her breathing. Before opening the door, she straightened the seams of her skirt and made a nervous sound in her throat. She slowly turned the doorknob and gently but tremblingly pushed the door open.

Jonell quickly turned around and picked up her music. "Hi, Miss Etta," she said and laughed. "Bet you thought I'd died, didn'cha?"

Miss Etta stood speechless, looking from one to the other, yet averting their eyes. "I'm sorry," she said finally, "if I'm interruptin' the audition, but I was worried about why you were takin' so long." She cleared her throat and played with the waistband of her skirt. "Then I heard the bell."

"That was unintentional," Mr. Riddick said. "I knocked it off when I was moving some things on the desk."

Jonell seemed surprised at that.

Miss Etta tried to smile but felt foolish. Trying to regain her composure, she said, "Then surely you've finished, Jonell."

"Oh yessum. I'm finished. I was just leavin'."

"Very well. We mustn't make Mr. Riddick get any farther behind. He's got a long drive ahead of him."

Jonell looked at Mr. Riddick and smiled. "Goodbye," she said hoarsely, turned and walked slowly to the door, looking back over her shoulder and making a gesture with half-closed eyes and a movement of her head which Miss Etta could only construe as provocative and obscene.

"Come on in, Mrs. Armstrong," Mr. Riddick said. "Now that Jonell is leaving, I can finish filling out her card and be on my way."

Miss Etta noted the unusual expression on Jonell's face as she walked out. Turning to Mr. Riddick, she said, "I'm sorry for bargin' in here like this, but I really didn't know what to think."

He quickly put his things together. "I need to write one or two more things on her card and then I'll be right with you."

She said she would wait for him outside.

He finished the card and pushed the chair under the desk. Miss Etta was looking out the back door when he joined her. He gently put his arm around her shoulder and pulled her to him. She was startled.

"Miss Etta, that student of yours has problems of a non-musical nature," he said and laughed.

She didn't know whether to laugh or not. What he said only intensified the sick feeling around her heart. She chuckled unconvincingly.

He waited outside while she got her things and locked the church door. She felt a deepening sadness as she did so but resolved to keep her composure. They walked to the parking lot and he helped her into her car.

"You're comin' by the house to pick up the cuttings I promised you, aren't you?" she asked as she settled herself in.

He obviously had forgotten. He looked at his watch, then slapped the top of the car. "Oh yes, that's right. Very well, I'll follow you home."

A few minutes later, as he put the cuttings in his car, Mabel Paradine watched from her front porch. Miss Etta wiped her hands with her handkerchief and followed him to his car.

He turned to face her, brushing the dirt from his hands. "Well, Miss Etta, it's time to say goodbye."

She shook her head and tried to smile. "Yes, I guess it is. And I'm so sorry to see you go, Mr. Riddick. I can't tell you how much your visit has meant to me. You've given me so much to think about. . . . And I sure hope you don't run into any bad weather." She felt her throat tightening and her eyes burning. She folded her hands together and moved them up and down, wanting desperately to put her arms around him.

"One of the nicest things about this judging business," he said, "is that you get to meet some very fine people now and then. You've made this job a lot easier than it would have been otherwise." He smiled and played with his keys. "I do want to thank you again for your generosity, your hospitality, and your understanding. I'm going to miss you and I'm going to remember you for a long time."

Without knowing she was doing so, she took the handkerchief from her blouse pocket and covered her mouth. He took a step forward and put his arms around her. Her body quivered as she tried to keep from crying. She couldn't talk for fear she'd say the wrong thing.

He stood back now with a hand on each of her shoulders and looked directly into her eyes. He smiled warmly. "Will you remember me?"

She shook her head, swallowed hard, and managed to say, "Oh yes! Yes indeed!"

"Remember what I told you at lunch today. And please try not to let the bad weather upset you."

He turned and got into the car. She stood with both hands to her chin, her lips quivering.

"Thanks again. I'll write you next week, Miss Etta. Goodbye and take good care of yourself."

As he pulled into the street, he waved. She stood motionless and numb, her hands clasped together, as he drove away. Even as he turned onto Laurel Street, two blocks away, and disappeared from sight, she still stood, her handkerchief squeezed into the palm of her right hand and both hands over her mouth. It was as though a ton of emptiness had driven her feet into the ground and she was powerless to move. She took deep breaths which, in spite of her extreme effort to compose herself, produced on each exhalation a soft, anguished sound in her throat.

10

"ETTA!" IT WAS MABEL, STANDING ON HER front porch with her apron on and her hair in curlers.

She turned, sniffed a time or two, dabbed her handkerchief to her nose, and walked slowly over to where Mabel was standing.

"Come on up and sit a spell," Mabel said as she motioned her to the other rocker.

Miss Etta slowly and carefully seated herself and straightened her skirt. "Thank you, Mabel. I think sittin' out here for a while is just what I need." She opened her handkerchief and smoothed it out against her skirt. "I feel so let down," she added, keeping her eyes on the handkerchief.

Mabel rocked back and forth and tapped her fingers on the arm of the chair. "I know, Etta. I understand how you feel now that the auditions are over." Then, in a happier voice, "From what I could tell, that Mr. Riddick was a mighty fine man." She stopped rocking long enough to remove a piece of broken fingernail. She watched Miss Etta as she did so. Then she gave a hearty laugh. "I saw him huggin' you out there a while ago before he left. Now wasn't that sweet of him!"

This cheered her up. She pulled in her chin and smiled. "Oh, Mabel, I do believe he was the finest judge we've ever had. He not only was honest, which is most unusual, but he was so kind and understandin' too. We had some wonderful conversations about music and teachin'." She looked straight ahead into the distance and squeezed her handkerchief into another little ball.

"I'm so glad, Etta. Lord knows you worked hard enough for those auditions. . . . How'd your students come out?"

She returned. "Oh, I guess they did all right, considerin' everything. But do you know I haven't even looked at their cards yet? I thought I'd wait till tonight or tomorrow. I'd like to have plenty of time to read what Mr. Riddick wrote."

The paper boy rode by on his bike and threw the paper heedlessly into the ditch. Mabel instinctively jumped up and hurried out to pick it up. She scanned the front page. When she came back to the porch, Miss Etta stood, straightened her skirt, and said she'd better get home.

Mabel laid the paper on the swing. "Etta, I was sorta hopin' you'd stay and eat supper with me. I'm fixin' to put a pan of biscuits in the oven and I've got some fresh cured ham. I thought I'd make us some scrambled eggs to go with the ham and biscuits. Now don't that sound appetizin'?"

Yes, it really did sound appetizing and comforting and just satisfying in every way. But she felt the need to be alone, to touch the sore spots and relive the week that was gone.

"Thanks, Mabel, that's awfully kind of you. But I really should be gettin' back to the house. I've got so much to do."

Mabel moved closer and took one of her hands. "Now Etta, you know that ain't so. The auditions are over and done with and you need to relax. And furthermore, you look like you ain't eaten in a month of Sundays."

She thought about last weekend and her desperation. She thought, also, about how little she'd eaten the past few days. What must she do? She patted Mabel's hand and smiled. "Mabel Paradine, what would I do without you? You know me so well." She chuckled. "And to tell the honest truth, I haven't eaten enough today to keep a bird alive."

Mabel put her arm around her waist and squeezed her. "I was hopin' you'd say that. I could use some company myself."

"Very well. But I must run to the house for a few minutes. I'll be right back."

On her way she picked up the paper. As soon as she had opened the front door, she remembered that Sophronia had been there earlier. It wasn't because the house looked any different than when she'd left this morning, but because the heavy lemony smell of furniture polish still emanated from almost every polishable surface in the house.

She took the stack of report cards she had hurriedly laid on the dining room table earlier and put them on her desk in the bedroom. As she did so, she hesitated and opened several and hastily read some of what Mr. Riddick had written. She thought about where he might be at this very moment. She recalled what he had said just before leaving and the way he had hugged her. She picked up the cards again, stood them on edge and evened the stack neatly. She looked around the bedroom, then out the window to Mabel's house. She thought about last Friday night and Saturday. If only she had known then how happy the following week was going to be it would have been so much easier to get through those two days. But now what was there to look forward to? The recital next Saturday night had not so far concerned her because of her preoccupation with the auditions. Now she tried weakly to work up some enthusiasm for it. But oh dear! How many more times could she stand to hear "Jukebox Jamboree," "The Space Walker," Clementi Sonatinas, Bach Inventions, and Chopin Waltzes? The best part was over. And Mr. Riddick was gone. There simply was no excitement left for anything else.

As she stood at the window, holding the cards upright in her hands, she felt the emptiness returning. She could see Mabel moving about in the kitchen. . . . Buttermilk biscuits, fresh from the oven, ham, and scrambled eggs, momentary surcease from her distress.

Only now did she become fully aware of the weather. Dark, loose clouds rolled and stumbled clumsily over one another just above the trees as they moved ominously to the east. White sprays of lightning, like tricks of the eyes, traced downward slices in the distance. The pink hue rimming the clouds meant wind. Now she remembered having heard someone saying something earlier about bad weather and a tornado watch. This reminded her that she had hardly read the paper or listened to the radio all week. Maybe she should call Mabel and tell her she wouldn't be coming over. The added concern about the weather intensified her dread of the coming night.

Mabel saw her and motioned her to hurry over. She held up both hands full of eggs to signal that supper was nearly ready.

She got her raincoat and umbrella and hurried as fast as she could. She smelled the fried ham even before she reached Mabel's porch. She called.

"It's open, Etta. Come on in and latch the screen."

The television was on in the living room. She stopped briefly to watch it. She put her things on the couch and went back to the kitchen. "Oh mercy, mercy!" she exclaimed as she stood in the doorway. "What a wonderful assortment of odors! I could smell the ham all the way outside."

Mabel was taking the biscuits out of the oven. "Well, I'll tell you, Etta, I just had this cravin' for some good ole breakfast food. I was over at the mall this afternoon and saw some of the prettiest ham in Sudley's I've ever seen. And from that very moment all I could think about was biscuits and scrambled eggs. You know, I almost never eat things like that for breakfast the way other folks do." She put the pan of biscuits on the table, reached over and got the coffee and poured it. "Sit down, Etta. That's your place over yonder."

Miss Etta sat down and opened her napkin across her lap. "Have you heard a weather report lately?" she asked.

Mabel sat down and motioned her to fill her plate. "Yeah, I have. As a matter of fact, we're under a tornado watch until four o'clock in the mornin'. There's been a bunch of tornadoes in Texas and one over around El Dorado. Accordin' to the weatherman a while ago, they're headin' in this direction."

She fumbled with her napkin. "Oh dear! Why do we have to have so many tornadoes? It used to not be like this. I can't help believin' all that foolin' around in outer space has somethin' to do with it. And it looks like they always come in the middle of the night, which means you can't get any sleep for worryin' about it."

Mabel seemed less concerned about the weather right now than about the biscuits, ham, and eggs. She nodded now and then to acknowledge Miss Etta's remarks and concern. She took a long generous swallow of coffee, refilled her cup and tendered the carafe to Miss Etta. She shook her head.

Mabel wiped her mouth and secured a curler that was loose. "We'll go in and watch TV as soon as we finish eatin' and see what the latest news is." She finished eating and, while sucking in on her teeth, eyed what was left of the ham and eggs, then filled her plate again.

"Have you heard any more from Annette?" she asked, lifting the cloth from the biscuit pan to see how many were left.

"No, I haven't. I owe her a letter but just can't bring myself to write. I'm so afraid I'll say the wrong thing. Now that the auditions are over maybe I can sit down long enough to compose a proper letter." Having said that, she seemed to have regained her appetite. She cut into the ham and put a piece in her mouth. "Oh, this *is* good ham, Mabel!" She took another biscuit and buttered it. "And nobody in Arkansas can beat you makin' buttermilk biscuits." She settled back in her chair. "This is so nice of you to have me over. Especially since the weather's so threatenin'. I just know I'm not gonna get any sleep tonight."

"Would you like to spend the night here with me? You know you're more than welcome."

"Oh, thanks, Mabel, but I don't think so. I think I should be in my own bed, even if I don't sleep."

Mabel sat back and drank her coffee more slowly now. Her face saddened. Her eyes were focused on something in the dining room. She put her cup down and looked at Miss Etta. She tried to smile. "You know what day this is?" she asked.

She wiped her mouth and quickly tried to remember why this day should be important. "Well, no, Mabel, right off hand I don't."

Mabel turned her empty plate around and around and stared at it. She cleared her throat. "It's twelve years ago today that Ernest passed away. Remember?"

"Oh, that's right!" She reached over and touched Mabel's hand. "Oh, dear Mabel, I'm so sorry. I should've remembered. This must've been a miserable day for you."

"Well, yes it was. And nothin' I could do helped to keep it from bein'. That's why I went to the mall. I just wanted to be around people." Then she reached over and patted Miss Etta's hand. She smiled. "But I feel much better now that you're here. And also now that I've stuffed myself like an old Arkansas razorback." She got up. "Would you like some ice cream or some Jello? I know that sounds kinda silly after ham and eggs, but I didn't know but what you might like somethin' sweet anyway."

She laughed. "Oh, goodness no! I'm so full right now I'm miserable. It was so good, Mabel." She got up and started to clear the table.

Mabel stopped her. "Now Etta, you go on in the livin' room and watch TV while I put these things in the dishwasher. I'll just be a minute."

"But Mabel, I want to help you clean up. After all, you did feed me my supper."

She turned and mockingly pointed her finger. "Etta, I ordered you outa my kitchen. Now go!"

She wiped her mouth and chuckled as she left.

Mr. Riddick took off his tie and threw it on the back seat. This was the best part of judging, leaving the arena and going home. It was true that he'd told Miss Etta about meeting some fine people along the way, but judging, all in all, was a tiresome business which required the greatest control over his feelings. Even though the Guild regarded him as a severe judge, he always made a special effort to be as personable as possible. There were always those teachers whose teaching upset him and left a deep, troubling feeling in his mind, and these were the ones he seemed to remember most after it was all over. He would like to be able to give all students good scores, but since this was not possible, he usually went away feeling frustrated and unhappy because he realized he'd left a lot of hard feelings behind.

It usually took about an hour to put the experience into perspective and sufficiently out of his mind. In the meantime, as he drove slightly over the speed limit down Highway 165, he mulled over some of what he'd heard and seen the past week. Most of the piano playing had been bad to mediocre, and this bothered him. . . . But then there was Miss Etta Armstrong! What a remarkable lady she was! He cared for her and was concerned about her. He cared for her because she was such a fine person, but he was concerned about her because she was so alone.

He knew how lonely old people can be. He'd known how lonely his grandmother Riddick had been the last ten years of her life, and he had seen at close range how his own dear mother had languished away following his father's death. Even as a child he had enjoyed being around older people, and after reaching adulthood he would often make a special effort to visit old friends or to stop by whenever he saw some old person who looked lonely, to strike up a conversation and before leaving to say or do something, no matter how trivial, to make him or her feel a little happier.

But Miss Etta was a special case. She hadn't just grown lonely; she seemed to have been born lonely. The more he thought about her, the stronger his feelings for her became. He remembered what she had told him about the tornado which killed her parents, and from other bits of information about her childhood following the tornado he tried to picture what her life had been like. He wondered, now, if any of her cousins were still living. She hadn't mentioned anyone except Jimmie Dale. Was he still living? If so, where was he?

He had hoped he could drive all the way home without having to stop to eat, but by seven-thirty his hunger had reached a point beyond compromise. Maybe a sandwich and a cup of strong, black coffee. Just south of Lake Village he decided to stop at the Western Wanderer, a new motel that looked clean and particularly inviting against a background of extremely dark and fearsome clouds. As he locked the car, he felt the uneasy weight and stillness of the air and stood for a moment in the premature darkness, looking back toward Montcrief. From every direction lightning split the sky, tracing haphazard, shaky figures like the markings of waterways and tributaries on a map. He thought about Miss Etta and, before entering the motel, said a short prayer for her safety.

After paying his bill, he took a few of the free mints from a bowl by the cash register, then walked to the front door and looked out, wondering what he should do. What he wanted most of all was to be home again and to spend the night in his own bed, and for this he was prepared to chance the weather. But at the same time, his concern for Miss Etta's peace of mind and safety had to be dealt with. He recalled how she had acted when he left. That had touched him more than she knew. Yet from a strictly practical viewpoint, how could he possibly help her? Was he being presumptuous to think she would feel better if he contacted her? When he would leave home before his mother died, he always felt a longing and an obligation to contact her as soon as possible, realizing it was as much for his own comfort as for hers. That's the way he was feeling now. Maybe he should call Miss Etta.

He went out to the car to get her phone number from his briefcase. At a phone in the lobby he dialed and waited. No answer. He dialed again. Still no answer. He walked out into the lobby where several people were seated around the television watching "Dallas," and waited for a minute or two before dialing again. Still there was no answer. He was disappointed but felt a little better for just having tried. He would drive on home and call her first thing tomorrow.

As he pulled out of the parking area and onto the highway, he felt something wasn't quite right. His car felt like it was somebody else's. Then it returned to normal and smoothed out evenly and reassuringly. He switched on the radio, hoping to hear a late weather report, but from one end of the dial to the other he was assaulted by a plague of country and western music. Assuming the strongest station was the nearest one, he set the dial and lowered the volume. He put one of the mints in his mouth, lowered the window, and headed south.

Watching television was a novelty for Miss Etta. She admittedly enjoyed it, yet she had no desire to own a set. It wasn't that she couldn't afford one but, rather, that she had strong convictions about the detrimental influence television had on people's lives. Her friends often reminded her that television was not entirely an instrument of the devil, that it could be educational and informative. They told her, also, usually with a special look and manner of speaking, that it could prevent or at least ameliorate loneliness. On several occasions Annette and Bob had wanted to give her a set but she had graciously but firmly declined the offer.

Mabel came in. With some effort she positioned herself in her recliner and raised the foot rest. "Anything I oughta know?" she asked as she adjusted her curlers again.

She wasn't sure what Mabel meant at first. Then, "Oh, no, nothin' other than what you told me a while ago. They've been flashin' that little warnin' message across the screen."

"What warnin' message? Did you say 'warnin''?"

"Yes. Why do you ask?"

Mabel adjusted herself to get more comfortable. She sucked a few times between her teeth. "They must've changed it from a while ago, then. The last time they said it was just a watch."

She wasn't as informed about weather talk as Mabel was. "You mean there's a difference?" she asked with more concern.

"Yeah. A warnin' means a tornado's been spotted somewhere nearby. Did they say anything about where it was?"

"No, I don't think so." She pulled out her handkerchief and dabbed at her mouth. She felt a growing weakness in her stomach. "Oh dear! What should we do?"

Mabel strained to reach a nail file on the end table. "Well, I guess nothin' right now. If things get worse they'll tell us what to do." As she smoothed off her nails, she watched Miss Etta out of the corners of her eyes.

Miss Etta stood and tugged at her skirt. "Oh dear. Maybe I oughta run home, Mabel, before somethin' happens."

Mabel motioned her back to her chair. "Sit down, Etta. You're as safe here as you'd be over yonder. Just try to relax, dear. . . . And anyway, I feel better you bein' here with me."

That was sweet of Mabel but she still wasn't fully convinced. She frowned as she slowly sat back onto the chair. She sat stiffly forward and played with her handkerchief, spreading it out on her lap and then refolding it.

Mabel got up and turned the volume down. "Let's just sit here and talk till 'Dallas' comes on. I want you to see it. Have you ever seen 'Dallas,' Etta?"

She shook her head.

Mabel was pleased. She smiled. "Oh, you're gonna like it," she said and sat back down. "And then at nine o'clock we'll watch 'Falcon Crest.' That's another good one. I watch 'em both every week that rolls around."

She only half listened as Mabel embroidered the plot of "Dallas" with personal observations and predictions about the outcome of events. The rest of her attention was given serially to thoughts of the weather, Mr. Riddick, and the coming weekend. From time to time she smiled deferentially or muttered a low and unacknowledged "Oh, my goodness," or "Well, I do know."

At a minute or two before eight Mabel got clumsily out of her chair and turned up the volume. She was clearly eager to see what new intrigues and passionate involvements were taking place. When the show began and the cast of characters was introduced, she made additional comments about each of them. She wanted to make sure Miss Etta knew enough about the show beforehand to enjoy it to the fullest.

No doubt about it, Miss Etta enjoyed "Dallas." She immediately became engrossed in the tangled affairs of the Ewing family and sat upright now and then to empathize with what was going on. All at once, without realizing it, she was thoroughly caught up in something other than herself and her own piano-playing world. She would have enjoyed it even more if Mabel had done less talking. Most of Mabel's remarks had to do with how she felt about certain of the characters. She laughed and admitted she liked J.R., even though most folks didn't, and couldn't help laughing at him even when he was being the meanest.

At twenty minutes past eight a severe weather bulletin startled them back to reality. According to the emergency announcement, a line of severe thunderstorms and tornadoes was moving eastward at forty miles an hour and persons in specified areas should seek immediate shelter. Montcrief was in the very center of the area most in danger.

"Dear Jesus!" Miss Etta muttered and jumped from her chair. She quickly took her umbrella and raincoat from the couch. Mabel stood, too, and looked nervously about the room.

"You ain't goin' home are you, Etta?"

She clutched the umbrella to her chest. Her face had grown colorless and her voice trembled. "I've gotta go home, Mabel. I've just got to," she cried.

Mabel hurried over to her. "Good God, Etta, that's the worst thing you could do. Now here. . . ." She tried to take the raincoat and umbrella from her. "Now you put those things down and let's you and me run to the hall closet. That's the safest place to be. . . . Come on, Etta, hurry!"

"No, Mabel, I can't stay." She moved her hands and body frantically. "I can't explain it now, but I've just gotta go home. I'll see you later." She opened the door and looked nervously in all directions.

An ominous, humid stillness lay darkly over the entire neighborhood. Above the giant oak and chinaberry trees along the street she could see the low-hung sky and against it the rampage of rolling and spiraling clouds like a numberless, smoky herd of preternatural creatures, demon-driven and pink-bellied.

Mabel stood anxiously behind her to close the door. "Well, if that's what you wanna do you'd better high-tail it on over there." She patted her on the shoulder. "And you be sure you close all your windows and doors and stay in your closet till it's over. And run you some water. And keep your radio on. . . . Now go on, Etta, and pray God we live through it."

She half turned her head and gave a pained look of understanding. Then she hurried mutteringly down the steps and across Mabel's yard to her own. A few feet from her steps she dropped the umbrella, tripped on it, and almost fell. She managed to catch herself. As she straightened, she looked upward once more. From every point in the distance a rapid succession of brief eruptions of lightning gave fleeting visibility to the turbulent sky and the helpless, unguarded landscape she knew and loved so well. The stillness was awesome. She found her key and with weak, trembling fingers managed to open the door. She latched the screen but before closing the wooden door stood for a moment and listened. Somewhere far to the west the stillness had been broken. The sound was indistinct but constant. She threw the umbrella and raincoat on a chair. She felt and thought she heard the accelerated pulsing of her heart. With one hand she clutched her chest and with the other closed the door and locked it. She nearly tripped again on the living room carpet as she hurried to the bedroom. She turned distractedly from side to side, too excited to know what to do first. How strange that in this state of mental and physical upheaval she should be singularly aware of the smell of lemon furniture polish!

She remembered the water. She plugged the bathtub and turned on the faucet, then went to the kitchen and filled three pots. What now, she asked herself as she squeezed her hands together. . . . The radio! She must set the radio to battery control in case the power goes off. She turned it on and found the local station. She heard the urgent last few safety precautions—do not go outside, stay away from windows and doors, secure yourself on the lowest level of your home and in the center of your house away from glass and movable objects. She suddenly became aware of the churning and discomfort in her stomach.

She couldn't remember how to adjust the radio to battery control. There must be a switch somewhere. She lifted the radio and her shaking hands almost dropped it. She muttered and talked to herself as she tried to find the switch. As she put the radio down, she thought she heard a distant train. . . . But that's not possible, she thought. The railroad tracks are miles away on the other side of town. . . . How strange! Surely that was a train! The sound grew stronger and nearer. . . . Oh, Jesus! she thought, that's a tornado! That's the way they sound!

The misidentified sound, like a long-delayed echo, matched in every respect a sound she had heard only once before when she was seven years old, the sound which preceded and would forever be associated with the most horrible experience of her life. The actual sound of a train would have been a pleasant thing to hear and would possibly have reminded her of the unique experience of her very first train ride or the exquisite thrill of many a ride that followed. But now that she knew what it was she was hearing, she could tell the difference with painful certainty. With shocking clarity for the brief duration of a flash of lightning it came forth from the coldest depths of her subconsciousness.

"Oh God! Oh God!" she cried aloud as she ran to the bedroom closet. "Protect me, Father, protect me," she prayed as she crawled inside and pulled the door shut. She frantically pushed the clothes as far as she could to either end of the closet and cleared sufficient space for herself. The thick, suffocating smell of mothballs ravaged the lining of her nose. She reached up and desperately pulled the clothes from both sides closer to her head and held the end of a coat about her face. She shook uncontrollably but couldn't cry.

She felt the slightest bit of comfort from the bit of light that slipped in beneath the door. She could clearly hear the radio. It was true, the announcer was saying, that a tornado had just touched down in the vicinity of Mont-Mart shopping center. She let out a scream and covered her mouth with the end of the coat.

She tried to push some boxes to the far end of the closet so she could lie down but was unable to do so. She positioned herself in such a way that she could lay her head on one of the boxes after pulling a jacket from a hanger and using it as a cushion behind her neck.

The awesome sound intensified. She heard the wind screaming and whistling like broken, repeated fragments of a pointless phrase as it lashed relentlessly at the front and sides of the house. The sound of the radio was now barely audible as the roar grew louder. Suddenly she realized the radio was no longer on and the light was no longer rimming the bottom of the closet door.

The total darkness added a new dimension to her fear. She prayed and listened. But now she could not hear the sound of the wind as before. The previous gale winds were now part of a greater force that shook the house and assaulted her ears to the point of making her scream. She reached over her head, pulled the coat from its hanger, and wrapped it clumsily about her head. With most of the sound now masked by the coat, she was able to think more sanely than before. She felt very close to God. She told Him so time and time again. Never would she have believed she could feel this way. Here she was, mercilessly at the point of death, yet for reasons beyond her grasp she was able to sense the danger and her relation to it in a nearly objective way. All at once, after a lifetime of fear and apprehension about dying, she felt an irrational peace and an overwhelming desire to be done with life. She was so innervated by the idea of final peace and happiness that she threw the coat from around her head and sat stiffly upright. She cried aloud, extirpating from her soul all the anguish, every vestige of her misery, "Take me, Father, take me! Take me now!" She leaned forward and cried bitterly.

Even as she cried, she heard outside the closet, above the furor of the wind, the random rattling of the windows and the multi-timbred sounds of objects of varying size and form being hurled against the house, sounds like percussion instruments making solo entrances in a cacophonous work by some demented composer. As she shifted her body and lay back against the wall to await God's response to her prayer, she heard something of immense weight hit the side of the house. She heard the glass shattered from the bedroom windows onto the floor and against the closet door and the increased volume of wind as it rushed inside. She screamed, pulled the coat from the floor and covered her head again. At that very moment, somewhere, in one of the abysmal and unfrequented repositories of her brain, a fear-induced nerve event sliced out her consciousness. She fell forward, both hands clasped in supplication at her chin, with her head coming to rest against the closet door.

11

Now it was all over. In the congested space of a few minutes it had come, devastated, and gone. The winds had ceased abruptly at nine-thirty and in their stead, like an encore topping off a superb performance, intermittent rains of torrential force had made it impossible for people to survey the damage. From time to time, someone with a flashlight or a lamp appeared at a window or a door, wanting yet dreading to see what had happened. Other than that, everything lay in total darkness.

After the rain stopped, there was a conspicuous absence of sound. The usual conglomerate drone of insects and the periodic accents of a dog's bark or the muted, sinister hoot of an owl, each a principal player in the orchestration for a typical Arkansas spring night song, had been temporarily quelled, excised from the score and replaced by an unsettling grand pause.

A pleasant coolness followed the rain. The sky seemed farther away than before. A dense cover of grey clouds lay like a worn or poorly made and overstuffed quilt stretched beyond its limit in every direction and pulling apart one frame from another, with an unintimidated moon taking advantage of every opportunity to break through at every strained seam.

In the ditches and the potholes and depressions along the black-topped street, water stood to capacity, reflecting with only the slightest distortion the efforts of the moon to work its way back from behind the clouds to center stage. Along the street and in a number of yards, trees lay uprooted or limbs lay strewn about like lurking wild creatures. A number of trees had fallen onto cars parked in the open, onto garages, or across driveways.

Lawns of new-green grass, which only yesterday were impeccably groomed, resembled dump sites with things normally kept out of sight now on chaotic display along with porch accessories, roof fragments, and dismembered screens, doors, and windows. Severed power and telephone lines snaked up and down the street and across yards like a child's senseless crayola markings, some emitting flashes of blue and white fire at fractured points and still others hanging from their moorings with deceitful innocence, ready to trip the careless or lure the unsuspecting and unwary to eternity.

Mabel was one of the first to emerge from hiding. She had managed, with the help of the faint moonlight coming through her windows, to find her flashlight. The radio, which she had kept at her side during the storm, she now placed on the kitchen table and raised the volume so she could hear it throughout the house. Her joints ached from her extended cramped position in the closet. The hair curlers by now were hanging loosely about her face. She brushed them away absent-mindedly. She moaned and limped from one room to another, satisfied for the most part that there had been no serious damage. When a neighbor across the street turned on his truck lights, she could see more clearly.

Now she realized she hadn't been completely spared. She saw her porch chairs splintered across the front lawn and into the street and an accumulation of other objects which she couldn't readily identify. As she turned the flashlight about the living room, she saw the broken glass from one of the windows. Some object, still hanging grotesquely from somewhere outside, apparently had broken the glass and spattered it throughout the room.

What about her car? She hurried to the kitchen and looked out the window. She knew right away that something out there had changed. She turned off the flashlight. As her eyes adjusted to the dark, she was able to see that something had indeed happened. The big chinaberry tree which had stood at the side of her garage was now uprooted and had fallen onto Miss Etta's house.

"Good God!" she cried aloud. "It's on Etta's house! Her bedroom!"

She grabbed the flashlight, hurried through the house, and started out the front door. The screen opened only a little. The swing had been blown off its hooks on one side and thrown against the door. She heard the screen tear as she pushed her way frantically out.

"It's Mabel!" someone shouted. "She's alive!"

Two neighbors hurried over.

"Are you all right, Mabel?" one asked.

"Yeah. At least I think so," she answered as she limped down the steps and started in the direction of Miss Etta's house.

"Where you goin', Mabel?" someone asked and grabbed her arm.

"Watch out, Mabel!" someone else hollered. "Those are live power lines there in your driveway. For God's sake, don't touch 'em!"

She stopped suddenly and swept the flashlight around the yard. "I see 'em, Albert," she replied nervously and went as fast as she could across Miss Etta's yard.

Three other neighbors were standing at the foot of the steps. They said they had been trying to work up their nerve to see why Miss Etta hadn't come out.

Mabel started up the steps but stopped suddenly. The porch was covered with the remains of the two rocking chairs, broken flower pots, plants, and potting soil. Most of the stands and tables where the plants had stood were scattered in pieces over the porch and in the yard, and the porch rail on the north side was collapsed with part of one of the rockers lodged across it. She clasped her hands together in a futile, sad gesture, kicked some pieces of flower pot away with her feet, and hurried to the door. She was out of breath.

She could feel the agitated pumping of her heart against her rib cage as she waited momentarily before knocking.

She knocked and called repeatedly, waiting each time to listen for some sign of activity inside. She peered through the door but could see nothing. She moved to the living room window but again could see nothing. She turned and made her way down the steps.

"I'm goin' roun' to the back," she said softly and shakily to the three women standing at the foot of the steps.

She knew she couldn't get to the back door by going around the south side of the house because of the fallen tree, so she made her way cautiously but hurriedly around the other side and to the back door. The screen had been torn off and lay against the bird bath several yards away. Miss Etta must have forgotten to latch it last night, she thought. She stepped onto the stoop and looked in. No sign of her. She knocked and called several times, reached down and picked up a rock and rapped time and time again against the glass pane. She waited each time and grew more and more terrified. Maybe she should try to get around to the bedroom windows where the tree had fallen. She picked her way slowly and more apprehensively around the back of the house. When she turned the corner, she looked over to her house and saw that her television antenna had been blown over and was hanging from the roof onto her living room window. This added to her distress.

She soon saw there was no way to get to the bedroom windows. She stood there, wringing her hands and crying, then inched a little closer, screaming again and again, "Etta! Etta! Are you all right? . . . Etta, it's me, Mabel! Are you all right? . . . If you are, come to the front door!"

Still nothing, not a sound of any kind from inside. Mabel lowered her head into her hands and cried, "Jesus, Jesus, Jesus, have mercy!" She stooped painfully over and picked up a short limb from the chinaberry tree, ran to the side of the house and started beating against the wall and screaming. "Etta! Fayetta, are you in there? Etta, it's Mabel! For Christ's sake, come to the door!"

By now she was hysterical. She moved back around the house as fast as she could and to the front porch where more people had gathered. She turned the flashlight aimlessly in all directions with one hand and fumbled the other hand nervously in her hair. "Dear Jesus!" she cried, "I know she's dead and I can't do a thing in this world to help her." With both hands on the flashlight, she leaned forward and beat it continuously against her knees. "I don't know what to do now. My God, what should I do?"

Lorena Satterfield came over and took her hand. "You mean you don't see or hear nothin'?" she asked and squeezed Mabel's hand.

Mabel looked directly into her face and her lips quivered. "Not a solitary thing," she answered and burst into tears.

Albert Simms came over. He had picked up a stick and was feeling his way cautiously, moving things out of his way. As he approached her, he put one of his hands on her shoulder and patted it. "Let's break down the door, Mabel. I don't see that we've got any other choice. . . . Come on and hep me."

"Which door do you plan to break down?" she asked.

"I thought we'd go in the front way."

"It'd be easier to get in through the back door, Albert. The screen's already blowed off and you can just break the glass, can't you?"

He considered the suggestion. "Sure, that would be better," he said. "Now Mabel, if you'll let me have your flashlight a minute, I'll go look in Etta's garage and see if I can find somethin' to break the glass with."

He took the light and soon returned with a length of metal pipe. He gave the light back to her and asked her to go with him.

She felt weak with fear. She tried to calm herself by taking deep breaths but found it hard to do. It was hard enough just to breathe. She almost collapsed when she considered what they might find inside.

"You all right, Mabel?" Albert stopped and asked.

She halted, gasped, and clutched her chest. "Well, no, I can't rightly say I am. I'm scared plumb to death and weak as pond water. . . . But you go on ahead. I'll follow in a minute."

Instead, he took her arm. "Here, let me hep you."

They made it to the back stoop. Albert went on up to the door but Mabel sat down and tried to calm herself.

"Wait a minute, Albert, before you break the glass. I've just gotta get hold of myself."

She took a few more deep breaths and with each one she felt the growing tightness in her chest. She sighed. "Go on, Albert. I'll be all right now, I reckon."

He took the flashlight, held it over his head, and directed it inside the house. There was no sign of life. Still he thought it best to knock on the door again just in case. He rapped his knuckles several times against the glass and waited.

"Go on, Albert! Break it! We're just wastin' valuable time."

He would break only one of the three glass panels and reach inside to unlock the door. He gripped the pipe, then laid it back down. Some instinct told him to try the doorknob first. He turned it. It opened. How strange! How unlike Miss Etta Armstrong to leave a door unlocked!

"My God!" Mabel cried. "What a small blessin'! Hurry, Albert! I think she's in her bedroom closet."

They called her name time and time again as they hurried to where she was. As they entered the bedroom, they both stopped short. Mabel gasped when she saw the shattered glass everywhere and the limbs of the chinaberry tree sticking out into the room. The curtains and shades had been mutilated and dislodged from their brackets.

"Dear Jesus!" Mabel screamed. "Albert, look at that!" She gave a frantic, quick look around the room before turning the flashlight on the closet door. She stood horrified before it, unable to move.

The first thing she felt was the extreme warmth and softness all around her. Then, as consciousness falteringly returned, she felt the nearness of the floor and the pain at the top of her head and in all her joints. Somewhere far, far away, there was a sound. What was it?

Where was she? She tried to move but seemed to be closed in on all sides. She slumped back onto the floor and tried to think. Slowly she became aware of the odor of moth balls. She heard the sound of someone's voice. She must say something! She made an effort to answer but nothing came out. Her mouth was a cavern of cotton and her tongue a hundred-pound weight tied at both ends by straps of steel.

She moaned in her more keenly felt discomfort and tried to raise her head and shoulders. As she laid both hands flat against the floor and tried to push herself up, her wrists and elbows collapsed and she fell forward once more. Again her head fell against the closet door and she felt the pain as though it had creased her scalp and lodged full-force in some forward lobe of her brain.

She raised her right hand to touch the pain and, as she put her hand back onto the floor, she touched a curiously shaped object. It was light and slightly cool. She fingered the shape feebly, put her hand to her face and realized her glasses were missing. They must be broken. She gave a desperate low groan. She tried to remember. There was something she needed to know that was filed away in one of the tiny vaults in one of the tiny rooms somewhere along that long, dark corridor of her brain, but she had forgotten the combination. She touched the glasses again and picked them up. Suddenly she remembered the sound of breaking glass. She must be careful, she told herself. She was pleased to find, upon running her fingers fearfully around the frame, that they were not broken. She pulled her left arm out from under her body, then, with both hands, arduously put her glasses back on.

All at once there was a rapid knocking and someone's voice much nearer than before. "Etta! Fayetta, are you in there? Etta, it's Mabel. For Christ's sake, come to the door!"

She stiffened and groped weakly for the doorknob. She managed to grab it but her hand slipped and she folded again onto the floor. She beat her fist against the floor and then against the door. "In here! I'm in here, Mabel! I can't get out!" It required all of her energy to get the words out, yet they couldn't be heard beyond the closet walls.

She made one last attempt to sit up but the extreme exertion only spent what meager strength was left. Her body went limp, like some deep exhalation, and filled the small space of her confinement like a piece of old clothing that had outlived its usefulness and was now carelessly wadded up and thrown away.

Mabel turned suddenly as Albert laid his hand on her arm. "You want me to do it?" he asked.

She sucked in a deep breath. "Naw, I'll do it." She moved closer to the closet, catching the end of her dress on one of the chinaberry limbs. Albert hurriedly cleared a path for her.

"Here," she said breathlessly, handing him the flashlight. "You hold the light." As she stepped toward the closet door, she felt and heard the broken glass snap and slide under her feet. She grabbed the side of the dresser to steady herself, stopped and turned around, hoping something Albert would do or say might help her. He only watched, waiting to do whatever might be necessary. She grabbed the knob with both trembling hands and slowly pulled the door open, heaving a pained gasp as she did so. Albert came closer and turned the light on the crumpled body on the floor.

Mabel quickly looked around again, then, without speaking, bent down and touched Miss Etta's neck. "Oh, my God!" she screamed. "Oh, dear God! She's alive! . . . Albert, she's alive!"

"Praise God! Thank you, Jesus!" Albert cried.

On her knees, with her arms around Miss Etta's shoulders, Mabel looked straight into her eyes and laughed hysterically. "Merciful, all-lovin' Jesus! You're alive, Etta!"

They tried to get her to stand up but she was unable to. Mabel held her close. Miss Etta sobbed and tried vainly to put her arms around Mabel's neck. Mabel cried, "Thank God! Thank God!"

Albert picked Miss Etta up, took her to Annette's bedroom, and laid her on the bed. Mabel sat down beside her and smoothed her hair. Miss Etta tried again to talk but couldn't.

Mabel turned to Albert. "See if there's any water. If there is, bring me some so I can wash her face. Maybe she drew some. Go see."

Albert returned with a towel and a kettle.

The wet towel felt good. Miss Etta lifted her right hand slowly and felt the pain in her shoulder as she touched Mabel's face. She smiled and cried at the same time.

Mabel smiled back, smoothing the soft grey hair into place as much as she could and running her fingers along Miss Etta's face. Then she straightened and gave a little groan as she felt her own soreness. "Etta, do you have a lamp or somethin' else we could use for a light?" she asked, moistening the towel again.

She motioned toward the other side of the house. "In the kitchen. . . . In the pantry . . . there's an old oil lamp . . ."

"Get it, Albert. We gotta have more light than this."

Miss Etta took Mabel's hands and tried to squeeze them. She started to say something but her lips went into a little spasm and she had to start over. "How bad is it, Mabel?"

Mabel thought for a moment, then chuckled. "Well, Etta, I really don't know right off hand, but I'll tell you one thing. You know that big old chinaberry tree of mine, the one out by the garage? The one you always said you liked and wished you had?"

She shook her head and raised her brows. "Yes, of course."

Mabel laughed again and patted Miss Etta's face. "Well, honey, you've got it. It's stickin' in your bedroom windows right now."

She covered her mouth with her hands. "Oh no! You don't mean it."

"Now would I be lyin' to you, Etta? It's true, honey. But there's no need to worry your little head about it, 'cause my insurance will pay for the damage."

She tried to raise herself. "Help me up, Mabel. I want to see what's happened."

"You sure you feel up to it?"

She sat upright and put her feet on the floor. "Oh yes! I've got to see what damage there is." She frowned as the pain nipped at her joints.

Albert brought the lamp. "Where you want it, Mabel?"

"Put it in yonder, Albert. She wants to see the tree I gave 'er," Mabel teased as she helped Miss Etta into the bedroom.

"Oh, merciful Father!" she cried as she saw the sight. "Look at all that glass! How will I ever get it all up?"

Mabel squeezed her shoulder. "Etta, you don't have a thing to worry about. I've done told you my insurance will take care of it. And for God's sake, don't you realize how lucky you are? How lucky we all are to be alive?"

She didn't answer. With her hands folded at her chin, she recalled how much she had wanted to die a short while ago. She must have been temporarily deranged. She realized also that she must have fainted. She could remember the sound of what must have been the tree hitting the house and the horrible sound of glass that followed, and then no further awareness until somewhere far, far away she had heard the anguished sound of those who were trying to find her.

"Are you all right, Etta?" Mabel asked her, seeing the strange look on her face.

Miss Etta raised her chin as though in defiance and stiffened her body in an attempt to regain her control. She smoothed her hair and adjusted her glasses, then smiled in spite of the pain she was feeling in a number of new places. "You're right. You're absolutely right," she said. "I must be thankful. And I am." The tears started again. "Yes, Jesus!" she threw her head back and cried to the ceiling. "I'm thankful!" She sniffed a few times and took Mabel's arm. "Can we go to the kitchen? . . . By the way, what time is it?"

"It must be about ten-thirty," Albert said.

By ten-thirty the work crews from the power company had arrived. The giant spotlights pierced the darkness everywhere with their intense, probing beams, discovering in many instances damage more severe than had been estimated earlier. The moon had now fully emerged, and only a few clouds of tattle-tale grey hovered motionless in the southeastern perimeter of the sky like abandoned offspring looking for some place to go.

The workers shouted to one another up and down the length of Holly Street and a man using a loudspeaker kept repeating a warning that all residents should go back inside their homes. There was extreme danger all about, he said. He announced, also, that the phone crews couldn't come to work until power had been restored, which meant that telephone service would probably be restored sometime tomorrow.

Mabel said she'd like to run over to her house for a few minutes. With the help of the spotlights she could get a better idea of her own situation. Albert said he'd stay with Miss Etta.

As Mabel let herself out the front door, a large group of neighbors was waiting apprehensively to hear about Miss Etta. She excitedly told them the good news and asked different ones what damage they had had. Their damage was relatively insignificant, they said, but some of the homes two or three blocks down Holly Street had been seriously damaged and two or three totally demolished. They asked if she thought it was all right to go in and see Miss Etta.

"Oh, good Lord yes! She'd love to see y'all. She's a little shook up right now but she's gonna be all right. I'm gonna run home for a few minutes to check on my damage but I'll be right back. Y'all go on in. Albert's in there with 'er."

As Mabel went from room to room, she instinctively flipped on switches and turned on faucets only to remember that there was no water or power. What about gas? Etta had a gas stove. She'd ask one of the crewmen later. She stood for a few minutes in the middle of her living room and tried valiantly to put her own values into perspective. Yes, they were all lucky to be alive. Relatively, her damage was slight. All except the antenna! She'd have that taken care of immediately!

One of the fellows working with the power trucks told her they still had gas. This made her happy. It meant that she and Etta could eat and make some coffee. Water! . . . Oh, my Lord! She remembered and hurried back to the kitchen, got one of the jugs she'd filled with water before the tornado, and left. She believed Etta had a stove-top coffee-maker.

"Be careful, Miz Paradine," one of the workers hollered as she started across the yard. "You've still got some live wires down there."

She thanked him and said she'd be careful.

Annie Pearl Massey, unaware that Miss Etta didn't know yet what had happened to her front porch, had told her how sorry she was and that she would be glad to help her reset or replace her plants. Miss Etta was standing at the front door with Annie Pearl, Albert, and two other neighbors when Mabel got to the front steps.

She set the jug of water down and got her breath before climbing the steps. When she flashed the light on the doorway, she heaved a big sigh. "Oh," she said. "I see somebody's already told you."

Miss Etta put her handkerchief to her mouth and nodded her head.

Mabel climbed the steps, kicked some debris from her path and stood looking around the porch. She shook her head. "Now ain't that disgustin'? All that work she put in them plants. And just look at 'em!"

"I told her I'd help her reset 'em," Annie Pearl said from behind the screen door. "I didn't know she hadn't been told yet."

Mabel opened the door and handed the water to Albert. "Here, take this, Albert. We're gonna make us some coffee." Then to Miss Etta, "You're in luck, little lady. The gas is still on. Ain't that wonderful?"

"Yes, it is," she said with genuine relief. "At least we can eat." She laughed, not too convincingly.

Mabel walked on in. "Come on, y'all. I'll make the coffee if Etta'll show me where the coffee pot is."

As they sat around the kitchen table drinking coffee, each of them seemed to sense the sweet comfort of being together. The oil lamp gave a mellow, faintly perfumed glow to their faces and projected distorted shadows against the high ceiling. To have looked out the window into the bright April night, one would never have guessed what had just happened.

Miss Etta held her cup in both hands and looked intently into it. "Y'all are so kind and thoughtful to come over. I don't know what I would've done if Mabel and Albert hadn't found me when they did."

"What I can't understand, Etta," Albert said as he poured himself another cup, "is why your back door was open. Mabel'll tell you, I came within a hair of breakin' the glass when somethin' just told me to try the doorknob first."

"You mean I left my back door open?" she asked, putting the cup down and looking at Mabel.

"You most certainly did, Etta," Mabel said. "I would never have believed it if I hadn't seen it with my own two eyes."

Miss Etta mentally separated herself from the others for a few moments as she tried to remember what she had done before the tornado. "Oh," she said finally, "I know why it wasn't locked. Sophronia leaves it open when she finishes cleanin' and in my excitement I must've forgot to lock it. I was so scared I didn't know what I was doin'."

"It's a good thing you didn't lock it," Mabel added and laughed. "I don't think you could've handled any more broken glass."

They all laughed.

When around midnight she assured them she would be all right, they left and promised to come back tomorrow to check on her and help her clean up. She thanked them and said again and again how much she appreciated them.

After she locked the door, she moved hesitantly back to the kitchen, the weight of the lamp she carried with both hands sending pain through her shoulders and elbows. She stopped in the dining room as she saw the box containing the gift from Mrs. Barrett. Setting the lamp down, she opened the box and gently ran her fingers over the folded cloth, then lifted one corner and brought the lamp closer so she could examine the skilled needle work that went into the border of gracefully joined garden flowers.

With her hands lightly resting on the tablecloth, she peered into the palely lit corners of the room and then at the trembling gold flame inside the lamp. It seemed like a year had passed when in fact it had been only several hours. The recollection of the past week was dulled now, a void of such meaninglessness and unreality as a dream might have. Even Mr. Riddick, who had been so real, now seemed far, far away.

She went to lock the back door and, as she did so, realized how foolish it was. She stopped for a few minutes in her bedroom and tried to adjust to the unnatural havoc of a tree sticking absurdly through her windows and the fractured window panes all across the bed, the desk, and the floor. This, too, was a dream, she thought. She must still be in some state of altered consciousness. Like something she had seen earlier in "Dallas," it was an extraneous event involving other people.

As she put the lamp down beside Annette's bed, she looked around the room and gave a sigh. She felt so unnatural here! She had avoided this room whenever possible. She didn't keep the doors closed, she didn't have to. Figuratively, she had closed and locked them long ago. She still remembered the anguish she had suffered after Annette left for college. And during the years that followed, how, after each of Annette's visits, the anguish had grown more acute as she realized the homecomings were growing shorter and farther apart and that Annette was moving farther away from her each time she came home.

And then the final blow that snapped the stretched and shortened bond, wedging Bob between them, further distancing them from each other. Her secret hurt went deeper than she wanted to admit, even to herself, and the more she tried to suppress or disguise it, the guiltier she felt. When Annette had returned later with Bob and still later with the children, it had never been the same. Now, as she pulled back the covers, she remembered not the last time Annette and Bob had slept here, but the sweet nights many years ago when Annette had slept here as a child, before Bob took her away.

How strange that she should be thinking this way! Maybe it was because she had come so close to death just now that she could have touched it by extending her fingertips far enough. The tornado had ripped off more than the roofs of houses; it had ripped off the thin veneer which usually cocooned these unpleasant thoughts.

How could she, who had always consciously and persistently tried to be righteous, have allowed her resentment for Bob to stain and torture her life? How senseless it all seemed now. What if she had been killed? All those ugly thoughts and feelings would have still been on her conscience like so many heavy stones to keep her soul from rising. She must do something. Yes, and soon! That's why God gave her this reprieve.

She blew out the lamp and got painfully into bed, knowing she was not going to sleep. She drew the cool, unfamiliar sheet over her, pulled it up to her chin and held it there with both hands. Actually, she didn't want to go to sleep. She felt, somehow, that all that had happened during the last several hours needed to be pondered more thoroughly than she'd been able to do so far. This terrible crisis had placed her in a defenseless position and had left her uneasy. It had temporarily obliterated her past, where during her frequent periods of distress she had taken refuge, and had made the future even more awesomely unappealing than it was before. She recalled the experience in the closet, the fervor with which she had asked God to take her life.

Then she recalled how Mabel and Albert had found her, and how her neighbors had been concerned and afraid she hadn't survived. This surprised her, though it shouldn't have. They had always cared about her. She remembered their outpouring of love and sympathy when Rupert died, and times of less serious crisis when they had hurried over to comfort her and help her through. There was that special occasion of Annette's wedding when Albert Simms, Clayton Massey and his two boys had bought paint and painted her house, and Mabel's husband Ernest and one of the boys from the plant had mowed and spruced up her yard for the event. She recalled, too, how different ones used to bring food over for no special reason except that they seemed to enjoy doing it.

She especially remembered Rowena Dobbins, a widow older than herself, a dear creature who had to use a cane to get about. She used to come over whenever she saw the last piano student leaving, most often bringing something she had just made in her ample spare time, and they would visit, drink coffee, and eat what she had brought. Rowena Dobbins was lonely also and she loved Miss Etta dearly. Now Miss Etta could remember only that someone had found Rowena dead after the postman was unable to get her to come to the door for a package.

She had not wanted to remember that Rowena's visits had become less and less frequent and had stopped altogether quite some time before she died. Nor had she wanted to remember how long it had been since her neighbors, with the exception of Mabel, had come to see her or done anything more than acknowledge her with a smile and a few words of greeting when they saw her. Oh yes, the tornado had left her defenseless! She felt this more surely than she was able at the time to substantiate reasonably. Something unpleasant lurked at the seabed of her consciousness and it troubled her and caused her to turn from one side to the other.

A little before three o'clock, she went to sleep. She didn't realize that the intense activity of her mind had ultimately subsided and that a comfortable position in her daughter's bed had relaxed her to a certain point where exhaustion had taken over and rest and sleep had come at last.

At four-thirty she was startled out of her sleep by the sound of a voice somewhere in the house and light coming from the next room. She tried to sit upright but the pain in her back forced her to fall back. Weakly and timorously she called out, "Who's there?" She listened but no one answered. Her hands trembled as she slowly and noiselessly slid from beneath the covers. As she sat on the edge of the bed, the pain and fright almost more than she could bear, she realized finally that the electricity had been restored and that the voice was coming from her radio which she'd forgotten about completely.

She laughed, in spite of her discomfort, and eased herself to a standing position. Holding on to the edge of the bed and whatever furniture was handy, she managed to get to her bedroom. Once again she looked in disbelief at the disruption of her little sanctuary and wondered how she'd ever get things back to normal. She listened briefly to the radio. The announcer was talking with some survivors from the Mont-Mart area. Their accounts of what had happened astonished her and made her cry. She turned off the radio and walked slowly about the house.

She turned on a kitchen faucet . . . a gurgle, two drops of precious water, then dry, hollow silence. She looked out the kitchen window and saw the detached screen door lying against the bird bath and her garbage can against her neighbor's fence, its contents strewn over the yard and clinging to bushes and the side of her garage. She walked to the front of the house and looked out the living room window. The street lights reassured her, yet they revealed a disorder like nothing she'd ever seen before. She opened the front door and stood bewildered, looking at what remained of her precious plants. She thought about how only yesterday she had given cuttings to Mr. Riddick. . . . Yesterday? . . . Surely not. It was a month ago at least! The thought that he had the cuttings was comforting.

The longer she stayed up, the better she felt. She turned on the lights in every room as an extravagant celebration of electricity. The light took away much of the horror and seemed to put things in perspective. Gradually she was able to reconcile herself to what had happened and to appreciate her deliverance. As she went from one room to another, she felt a love for the old house stronger than anything she'd ever felt before. She stopped now and then to touch some piece of furniture and run her gnarled fingers tenderly over it or to look with new appreciation and heightened perception at a picture or some treasured piece of crystal.

She took the tablecloth Mrs. Barrett had given her and held it to her face, then cleared the table and spread it over it, pulling at one point or another to make it hang evenly. It fit perfectly and looked beautiful. After putting the other things back on the table, she went to the kitchen.

She was so happy and so glad to be alive, yet something still troubled her. It was as though she were pacing the worn floor of her own soul, cautiously avoiding one particular spot, one particular plank beneath which she sensed a latent, unspecified peril. She wasn't sure what the peril was, but she knew intuitively not to walk there, to avoid stepping on that spot just as she avoided going into Annette's room or stepping on that loose sidewalk slab in front of her house.

As she looked out the back door, it occurred to her that she hadn't read her Bible last night. That's what she needed; she must clear her mind and reestablish her moral priorities. Reading her Bible almost always helped her do that. She carefully wiped the Bible to make sure there were no glass shards on it, then went into the living room and, before sitting down, took another look out the front door and thought how strange everything looked in the innocent first light of day.

It would be fitting, she thought, to read some of the psalms. They could best express her feelings, her joy at being alive, her gratitude, her praise. She held the book with her left hand and laid the other hand lovingly on top of it, smoothing her fingers back and forth across the soft, scarred leather binding and feeling, as she always did, that she was touching God. She pressed it tightly to her chest and involuntarily uttered a weak, desperate sound that could have come from pain just as well as from joy. She opened it to the Book of Psalms.

When she wasn't sure what she wanted to read or what she thought she ought to read, she would often play a little game with God. She would select a page at random and, if what she found on that page happened to have special meaning for her at that particular time, she would construe it as God's way of speaking directly to her. Sometimes the results were astonishing! At other times, when what she found was less than appropriate, she would read and reread the verses, trying to find new meaning or deeper insight, while at the same time adjusting her own thinking and reassessing her real needs and feelings in order to lessen the disparity between herself and what was "revealed" to her. The fact that the book often opened of itself to some of her favorite scripture either did not cross her mind or, if it did, it didn't affect the way she felt or the way she played the game.

In her exalted state of mind, the words visibly became three-dimensional and leaped from the page onto her brain with computerized precision. Like pointed, razor-sharp pellets, they entered smoothly and cleanly and landed right on target, energizing every single circuit of her comprehension. She read for about half an hour, then prayed and recommitted her life, as she did daily, to God's keeping.

By now she was so relaxed she felt like closing her eyes for a few moments before fixing her breakfast. Still holding her Bible, she leaned her head back and put her slippered feet up on the hassock. Every part of her body seemed to be at the right place. The old velour-covered chair with its worn spots and strategic lumps and depressions and the matching footrest Annette had given her many years ago were like a comfortable, tried-and-true mold made perfect after years of experimentation and adjustment and now conforming faultlessly to her small, weary body.

The sound of people talking out front awoke her a few minutes later. The sun was up and flooding the house. The rays coming in the back door and the kitchen windows had permeated the dining room, had entered the living room, and were laying silver highlights on the crystal chandelier.

She got up with a great deal of effort and an equal amount of pain, stood at the door and fingered her disheveled hair back into place as well as she could, and unwittingly checked the top button of her robe. She looked forlornly at what was left of her rockers and the broken plants, flower pots, and dirt, then made her way through the door and onto the porch, where she stooped over, holding onto the banister with one hand, and picked up a few of the plants that looked salvageable. She had started back inside with them when she saw Mabel and Albert standing near the fallen chinaberry tree. After taking the plants inside, she went back to the porch, down the littered steps, and over to where Mabel and Albert were.

They were happy to see one another.

"D'you sleep, Etta?" Mabel asked.

"Oh yes, I did," she lied without realizing she was doing so. She pulled the collar of her robe about her neck. "How long y'all been up?" she asked.

"Near 'bout all night," Albert said.

Mabel was looking at an armrest from a rocker and seemed puzzled. She threw it down with a grunt and wiped her hands on her apron. "I ain't been up too long," she said. "Me and Albert've been lookin' at some of the damage further down Holly Street. Dear God, some of them folks got hit bad. I didn't realize how lucky I was till I saw what they went through."

Albert told her in more detail about the Anderson and Willis houses two blocks away and the way even the sidewalks had been displaced.

"Albert's go'n' help us, Etta," Mabel said. "Bless his soul, he's go'n' saw down my poor old chinaberry tree and clean it out for us."

"Oh, how nice, Albert," Miss Etta replied. "That's a great load off my mind," she added and reached out and shook his hand.

Mabel watched them both, then said, " . . . And?"

Miss Etta didn't know what she meant.

Albert laughed. "Mabel means and then what am I gonna do after that. I told her I'd fix your windows for you, and I believe me and my grandson can fix that broken porch rail. The only thing is I won't be able to do it till Monday or Tuesday. That all right?"

She squeezed both of his hands and tears filled her eyes. "Oh, Albert, that's wonderful! I can't tell you how much I appreciate it."

Mabel stepped over and touched Albert's arm. "Ain't he a sweetheart, Etta, for bein' so good to us old widder women?"

She smiled and wiped her eyes. "Albert's always been a good neighbor." She gave her nose a little blow. "By the way, Albert, how are things at your place? Did you have any damage?"

"Not much to speak of. Just some limbs from my pecan trees and one of my awnin's blew off a back window."

Mabel turned and peered in every direction. "Didn't nobody but me lose an antenna?" she asked and looked several houses down at the south end of the street. All at once she pointed in that direction.

"Lord, y'all! It's the telephone men! Look! Oh, thank God! Now we can rejoin the world."

It was understandably a happy turn of events. The three of them hurried out to the sidewalk and watched the crews as they hit the ground and started setting up their equipment. Mabel hollered at them and told them how glad she was to see them and to stop by for coffee.

She turned to Miss Etta. "Speakin' of coffee, have you had breakfast, Etta?"

She shook her head. "I was just fixin' to cook when I saw y'all out here."

Mabel put an arm around her shoulder and squeezed her. "Wanna eat together? What about you, Albert? You eaten yet?"

"Yeah, long time ago."

"What about it, Etta? . . . Lord God, I feel so good I just wanna be with folks." She squeezed Miss Etta closer to her. "And there ain't no way I can tell you how happy I am that you're all right. I don't know what I would've done if . . . " She couldn't finish.

Miss Etta considered the alternative. "Oh yes! That would be such fun!" She laughed so hard her frail body shook. "Your place or mine?"

Mabel thought for a moment. "What say we go to my house? I've still got some more of that good ham we had last night. . . . Lord, Etta, just think. Seems like a month ago, don't it?"

They made their way slowly and cautiously to Mabel's house, holding hands like two little girls getting ready to play. "Oh," Mabel said suddenly, "did you know the water's on, Etta?"

12

THE ACTIVITY AND EXCITEMENT HAD ALREADY peaked on Holly Street by seven o'clock. Everything was out of proportion. This was surely no ordinary Saturday morning. People had to shout if they wanted to be heard over the noise the power saws and bulldozers were making. In the 100 block of Holly Street, there was little or no talk of damage or loss. Those folks were too happy to have come through the storm so well.

Miss Etta and Mabel walked over to the street and watched two crewmen working on a telephone pole.

"How soon y'all go'n' have it fixed?" Mabel asked.

" 'Fore long, m'am," one of them said. "See that big old oak tree down yonder?"

"Yeah."

"That's what caused the trouble and's takin' so long. But we'll have it fixed any minute now."

"Thank you," she said and moved back to where Miss Etta was standing. Looking up at her roof, she frowned and bit her lower lip. "Oh, look at my poor old antenna. I don't know how I'm gonna live without my TV."

Miss Etta was remembering "Dallas" and wondering how it would feel to have a television. "I know, Mabel. I'm so sorry. Maybe Albert can fix it. You reckon?"

Her mind was somewhere else. "What? . . . Oh, no. I'll have to have that fellow from the store. Lord, I hope he can fix it Monday."

The two of them stood for a while, watching people cleaning their yards or looking at the damage. Mabel turned to Etta and asked, "What you go'n' do now?"

"I don't know. I think I should try to do a little cleanin' up." She stopped and looked far ahead. "I don't know where to start."

"I wouldn't, Etta. I'd wait if I was you. You know when Albert moves the tree you gonna have more glass and mess to clean up. And anyway, didn't Annie Pearl say she'd help you?"

"Yes, I know. But Mabel, I can't ask her to do that."

"You're not askin', Etta, for Christ's sake. She's volunteerin' to do it out of the goodness of her heart."

She put her hands to her mouth again and tightened her lips. "Oh dear, I feel so helpless."

Mabel grabbed her hands and shook them. "Stop that, Etta! For God's sake, stop tryin' to be so self-sufficient. You've shut yourself off from people so long you've forgotten how important they are and how much you need 'em."

She felt herself growing weak. Mabel had put her foot down on that loose plank! Determined not to lose control, she took out her handkerchief, then decided not to use it for fear she'd give herself away. She raised her chin. "Is that what you think?"

"Yes, that's exactly what I think. Fayetta Rose Armstrong, you don't fool me for a minute. You never have."

She pulled the sash of her robe tighter. "It sounds like I'm about to hear a lecture."

Mabel laughed and gently touched Miss Etta's face. "No, dear, I ain't gonna lecture. But I do wish to Heaven you'd stop makin' yourself miserable."

This startled her. Not the thought itself but the fact that Mabel had said it. She knows! She pressed the handkerchief to her lips and tried not to let go.

Mabel continued after a pause. "You saw how concerned everybody was about you. You saw how much they all care. If this surprises you it's only because you ain't seen nothin' like it for so long, and that's because you ain't given folks a chance to show you. You can't understand how folks can be so thoughtful and carin', can you? Admit it, Etta. It's taken a damn tornado to wake you up!"

"Oh Mabel!" she cried and turned away. "Please don't scold me. Not now. I'm too confused."

"I know you are. But honey, I'm just tryin' to get you to see you're not foolin' nobody but yourself." She reached down and picked up a big nail, studied it for a moment, then put it in her apron pocket. "You might think it's none of my business to talk to you this way, but it is. It's as much my business as it was for me to find you and get you out of that closet last night. You know how much I love you, Fayetta. And surely I ain't the only one, for God's sake. There're lots of people that love you just like I do, but outside of me you don't have nothin' to do with nobody much. And you wouldn't've had anything to do with me if I hadn't pushed myself on you all these years."

Miss Etta felt an imminent emotional deluge. She held the handkerchief tightly over her lips and made suppressed sounds of anguish, breathed deeply several times and tilted her quivering chin in a last, futile gesture of control. "Could we go inside?" she asked softly.

They went to her house and through the cluttered porch into the living room. She motioned Mabel to sit down, then lowered herself with lingering discomfort into the old chair where she had been so comfortable a short while ago. For a while, neither of them said anything. Mabel shifted around uncomfortably in the chair, stretching her plump hands out, studying them, pushing the cuticles back and checking each nail for rough edges. Miss Etta had stretched her handkerchief out across her lap and was smoothing it absentmindedly. After a while, she cleared her throat. Mabel had been watching out of the corners of her eyes as though wondering when she was going to say something.

"I'm embarrassed, Mabel," Miss Etta said finally. "I feel so vulnerable. Ever since last night I've had the strangest feelin'. You're right, you know. About me, I mean. I know it's my fault that I've been alone all these years, but I can't help it if I want to be alone so much of the time. It's just my nature. You can understand that, knowin' how I was brought up and . . . and about Mamma and Papa, and Uncle Lester. . . . And Rupert." She stopped and looked directly at Mabel. "Is that so wrong? Have I committed some terrible, unpardonable sin?"

"Of course not, honey. I know why you're the way you are. And God knows you don't have to apologize. Certainly not to me."

"There are other reasons, too," she added, pulling at the corners of the handkerchief. "I've always felt, ever since I was a child, that I'm a better person when I'm by myself. I feel better, spiritually."

"Don't you believe lots of other people do, too?"

"I suppose so. But you do understand. It's true." Then she covered her mouth again as though she had said or done something wrong. "Oh, Mabel, I've never wanted to complain about my troubles. I've always tried not to burden other people with my problems. I like to think that with God's help I can handle them. But somethin's happened. I guess, like you said, the tornado's made me take a closer look at myself." She folded her hands tightly together.

"And you bein' a musician and all," Mabel added, "it's only natural for people like you to wanna be by themselves a lot. I surely ain't blamin' you for that." She pulled down on her skirt. "Now Etta, we both know that after all's said and done, nothin' I say's gonna change you anymore'n anything you say's gonna change me. Least, not at our ages! I just wish, though, you'd stop shuttin' people out of your life. You don't have to be with 'em every blessed minute of every blessed day, but Fayetta, I know how much better you'd feel. You could still have your own privacy. You wouldn't have to give it up."

She smiled weakly. "I know. And I'll be perfectly honest with you, Mabel. That meant so much to me last night when you, Annie Pearl, and the others came over to be with me. I think it was seein' how happy y'all made me that started me thinkin' seriously about myself."

Mabel got up from the chair and moved over to the couch, then put both of her hands gently on Miss Etta's. "One more thing, honey, then I promise to shut my big mouth." She leaned back and pulled her skirt out from under her. "Look, Etta. All of us old folks live in constant fear of dyin' or seein' those we love die. And the older we get, the more we dread it. It seems to me that at some point in your life you must've figured you had a way to avoid all that. Well, maybe not all of it, but some of it, anyway. I believe you must've made up your mind that you'd rather not have friends than to suffer every time one of 'em died."

Miss Etta lowered her head with a heavy sigh and squirmed herself into another position in the chair.

"I wonder, though," Mabel continued, "did you really help yourself or did you make yourself more miserable?" She leaned over and took one of Miss Etta's hands. "Etta honey, I know how much you've been hurt. I've known for a long time. But don't you see, Fayetta? What you've done instead is you made a life for yourself where every single day has been miserable. And you couldn't do nothin' about it. Teachin' them kids day in and day out ain't never go'n' change that! Them kids ain't no substitute for real friends, folks your own age." She squeezed Miss Etta's hand and looked deeply, tenderly into her eyes. "Am I right?"

At first she couldn't speak, nor could she look directly into Mabel's eyes. She frowned and pressed her lips together to keep from letting go. Mabel took Miss Etta's chin in both hands and lifted it, smiling. Miss Etta turned her eyes to meet Mabel's. As soon as their eyes met, she lost control, threw her arms around Mabel's neck and wept uninhibitedly.

Mabel had been gone about twenty minutes when Albert Simms started cutting away at the chinaberry tree. Miss Etta had just started brushing her hair when she heard the erratic glissandos and the spastic, sputtering screams of the power saw. At first she was startled, but when she heard Albert and someone else talking, she realized what was going on. She walked to her bedroom door and watched as little by little they dismembered the tree and pulled the limbs from her windows. Each time the limbs were pulled, more glass shattered into the room. She couldn't watch long because it made her too nervous.

She was making up the bed in Annette's room when the phone rang the first time. She had been lost in thought, mulling over what Mabel had told her, and the shrill incisive first sound frightened her. It was Velma Mayfield. They had all been worried and wanted to make sure she was all right. The Mayfields lived several miles north of Montcrief and had not had any damage.

It was the first of a series of calls from friends who had been trying unsuccessfully to contact her for hours, most of them not aware that the busy signal they heard each time did not mean someone else was on the line. Each time the phone rang, she complained aloud to herself about the annoyance it was causing, yet she was excited and happy that people cared so much about her. Brother Butler, her pastor, and several others promised to come by later today to see her.

Annie Pearl Massey came over as soon as she saw that Albert had finished removing the tree. After she and Miss Etta had changed the bed and cleaned up all the glass, chinaberry fronds, and other debris from the bedroom, they cleaned the porch. Albert had come inside to measure the windows and Miss Etta was with him when the phone rang again.

"Miss Etta Armstrong?"

She tried to identify the voice but couldn't. "Yes, this is she."

"Hello, Miss Etta. This is James Riddick. I'm calling to see how you are. I heard about the tornado last night."

The sound of his voice instantly closed the gap which the tornado had put between them. Now she felt fully awake. "Oh, Mr. Riddick! How wonderful it is to hear your voice! And how thoughtful of you to be so concerned. . . . Well, I'm fine, thank you. And how are you? Did you have a pleasant trip home?"

"I'm not at home, Miss Etta. I spent the night at Lake Village. I had some more car trouble."

"Oh, my goodness! I'm so sorry, Mr. Riddick. I know how eager you were to get home. Was the trouble serious and are you havin' it tended to?"

"I'm afraid it's more serious than I thought. I'm in quite a predicament. I couldn't find anybody here who would work on it, so I called the fellow who worked on it the other day in Montcrief. You know, the Manning fellow, and he agreed to come over later this morning to see if he can fix it. If not, he's going to have to tow it back to Montcrief."

Her immediate, fleeting, guilty reaction was one of delight. "Oh, Mr. Riddick, I'm really so sorry. What a shame! Where were you when it happened?"

"Just a few miles south of Lake Village. I was lucky enough to get a ride back here to the motel. I shouldn't have tried to drive home in such bad weather, anyway. . . . But look, Miss Etta, I'm really calling about you. Did you have any damage? Are you really all right?"

She mustn't say too much. She had survived, no need to relate all the horrible details. She cleared her throat as she sat down on the little phone chair. "I'm just fine, thank the good Lord. It was pretty frightenin'. Well, actually it was terrifyin', as you might well imagine. I didn't have too much damage. Well, a little bit. I lost all of my little plants on the front porch. You know, the ones I gave you cuttings from. I surely am glad I gave them to you."

"What a shame! I'm so sorry, Miss Etta. Are you sure you weren't hurt?"

"Oh no, Mr. Riddick. I'm just fine. Really I am." She cleared her throat again and hoped God would forgive her for not telling the entire truth.

"Well, I'm very happy to know that. Oh, incidentally, would you like to have those cuttings back? You could, you know, if I have to come back over there."

"Oh, my goodness, Mr. Riddick! I gave those cuttings to you and I want you to keep them." She enjoyed thinking about her little flowers growing in his garden, creating some kind of sweet, private bond between them. "I still have a few left. More than enough to keep me busy, I daresay," she added.

"I'll let you know how mine make out. If they do well, I'll give you some of my cuttings one of these days. Does that sound fair enough?"

She chuckled happily. "Oh, what a lovely thing to say! . . . Well, I do hope Mike can fix your car so you can get on home. I know how frustratin' it is and how eager you are to be back in your own place. It was so thoughtful of you to call and I do appreciate it so much. Remember, now, if Mike can't fix your car and has to bring it back over here, you be sure and let me know, you hear? I certainly want to know if you're back in town so I can do whatever I can to help. Will you promise to call me?"

He laughed. "Yes, I promise. But you can help me now by saying a little prayer that he doesn't have to tow it in. Nevertheless, I wanted to make sure you were all right. Actually, I called last night but couldn't get you. I feel better now. And again I want to thank you for all you did for me this week. And thank the other ladies for me. I hope we can keep in touch. I'll write as soon as I get my life back together. Take good care of yourself and be happy. Goodbye and God bless you."

She realized as soon as she hung up that Mr. Riddick had not only closed the gap between the tornado and the week before, but had built a bridge over the otherwise uncrossable chasm to the future. As she disinterestedly busied herself about the house with chores of no urgency, she found herself thinking more and more about her students. She realized she hadn't yet looked at their cards. Before long, she was thinking about the recital next Saturday. Only one week away! So much yet to do! She must remind her students of the rehearsal Thursday evening, and she must contact Mr. Glendennin and have him tune the piano. She must get the program to the printer and hope he'd have it ready by recital time. It was so easy to resume the little tedious burdens of her life.

She found it all so reassuring. Admittedly, although the tornado had knocked her off balance, the attention she was getting was satisfying. But more than anything else, she wanted to get back to normal. To what extent the tornado had jeopardized her independence and privacy by leveling her defenses and putting her weaknesses on public display, she could not determine right now. Nor did she want to think about it. In her more lucid moments, she could see a striking parallel between what the tornado had done to her home and what it had done to her life. But it was too soon to see things in any kind of uncluttered perspective. She mustn't try to walk where there were yet no tracks.

She knew she must keep busy or collapse. She spent some time making a list of the things she needed to do for the recital and decided, first of all, to call Mr. Glendennin. She wished there were someone else she could get to tune the piano. Mr. Glendennin was a nice old gentleman, but he could no longer hear very well, he was too nervous and weak to do any kind of repair work, and he usually seemed more interested in visiting than in tuning the piano. She had learned years ago to stay out of the room when he was working on her piano.

She was able with some difficulty to get him to understand who she was and why she was calling. He seemed confused but said he'd take care of the piano next Friday so it would be in good shape for the recital.

Now would be a good time to start looking at the students' audition cards. As she returned to the living room, she could see in the bright sunshine that there were still some shivers of glass mixed in with the cards. After she had gone outside and wiped each card individually, she returned to her comfortable chair and began reading the comments Mr. Riddick had written. She simply could not keep her eyes open. Somewhere about halfway through the stack of cards, she dropped off to sleep, the unopened cards resting on her knees.

She jumped and knocked the cards onto the floor when the phone rang. She felt the pain and stiffness in her legs all over again as she swung them from the hassock onto the floor and started to the bedroom. She failed to negotiate the edge of the living room carpet with her right foot and tripped, but managed to keep her balance by grabbing onto the door facing. The shrill persistency of the phone suggested, as difficult passages in her pieces used to do, that someone was angry with her.

She breathlessly took the phone with one hand and dug the fingers of the other into her lower back muscles. "Hello." She didn't sound like herself. She cleared her throat, gave her diaphragm an extra push, and said again, "Hello."

There was a brief delay at the other end. "Hello. . . . Mother? Is that you?"

She quickly grabbed the phone with both hands and squeezed it close to her ear. "Annette! Oh, Annette! It's really you!" She hadn't wanted to cry but couldn't help it.

"Mother? Mother, are you all right? I've been so worried about you. . . . Mother, are you still there?"

She checked herself. This was no time for tears. "Yes, dear, I'm still here. Oh, Annette, I'm so happy to hear your voice."

"And I'm happy to hear yours, Mother. I've been trying to call you all week. And last night, when I heard about the tornado, I tried for hours to get you. Tell me honestly, Mother, are you all right? Was there any damage?"

"I promise you, dear, I'm fine. It was a very bad experience, Annette, and there was some damage, but I was very lucky. . . . Oh, my dear child, I'm so happy you called. And mother apologizes for not writin' but I've been so busy, dear. We had our auditions this past week and I hardly had time to catch my breath. . . . Tell me all about yourself and the children . . . " She almost couldn't say it. "And Bob. How's everybody?"

"We're all fine, Mother. We've got all the things we don't need packed and we're all excited about going to Germany."

She offered no response. Better to say nothing than the wrong thing.

Annette continued. "Bob'll be through next Thursday, so he plans to visit his folks in Charleston for a few days. Sharon and Kathy are going to stay with me." She hesitated. "And Mother, I have a surprise for you."

Her wrists ached from holding the phone so tightly, and she was weak with apprehension. "Oh you do, do you? I surely hope it's a nice one."

"I think it is. You see, we're not going to be leaving for Germany until the middle of August. We're sub-letting our house and have to be out next week. Bob and I've discussed things and would like to come stay with you a while. I thought if it's all right with you, I'll come with the girls next week and Bob can come later. Is that all right, Mother?"

She quickly determined, as soon as Annette said Bob would be coming later, that she would not let her petty resentment spoil things, and she was surprised that it was so easy to do. "Oh, my dear!" she cried. "Is it all right! You know perfectly well it's all right. It's wonderful! Oh, Annette, that's the best news I've had in ages. Tell me again, dear. When did you say you were goin' to get here?"

"We'd like to come next week, Mother. I thought we'd leave here Wednesday morning and get there sometime late that evening. Are you sure this isn't going to inconvenience you? Do you have things to do?"

"Oh, Annette, nothin' in this world is more important to me than seein' you and the children. Now, I'm havin' my recital next Saturday evenin' but that won't matter. . . . Oh, Annette, that means y'all will be here for the recital, doesn't it?"

"Yes, Mother. That will be fun. It'll be like old times. I'm sure Sharon and Kathy will enjoy hearing the other kids play. . . . Now, is there anything else you need to do?"

"Nothin'. Nothin' at all. Oh, dear child, hearin' from you has given me a new lease on life. Everybody's been so good to me, Annette. It reminds me of when your father died. . . . Look, dear, I'll get your room all ready and I'll borrow Mabel's hide-a-bed for the girls or maybe they can just stay at Mabel's. But no matter. Y'all just come on and we'll work out these little matters after you get here."

"That's right, Mother. There's no need to worry about anything. But Mother, that's only part of the surprise."

"Only *part* of the surprise? You mean there's more? Oh, my word, I don't think I can stand much more. What in the world are you talkin' about?"

Annette laughed. "We want you to spend Christmas with us in

Germany. You've never been to Europe and I remember how many times you used to say you wanted to go. I know this is going to shake you up for a while, but we really want you to do it. You can leave in November sometime and come back after the first of the year. Doesn't that sound exciting?"

She had sat down. By now, she was too excited to know what to say or do. She responded in typical fashion. "That sounds perfectly wonderful, dear, but you know I can't be away from home that long. And you know there's my church work and my students."

"I knew you were going to say that, Mother. Those are simply not valid reasons, and I want you to think very seriously about what I've said. We'll discuss it when I get home. In the meantime, don't go buying a lot of food and things before we get there. You and I can take care of all that later. . . . And Mother, I'm so happy you're all right. And just in case you don't know it, I love you very much. . . . Now remember, we should get there around four o'clock Wednesday afternoon. If for any reason we have to change our plans, I'll call you. . . . Bye-bye, Mother."

13

ANNETTE'S PHONE CALL LEFT HER IN A MILD state of shock that lasted for over an hour. She walked from room to room, smiling, squeezing her hands together and talking softly to herself. The house and everything in it suddenly took on new meaning. The sound of Annette's voice and the joy of knowing she would soon be home spread like a delectable fragrance from one part of the house to another, into every corner and lightless cranny like long-deterred sunshine at last gaining access, touching things that had lain for years in dreary seclusion and neglect and stirring them back to life and purpose.

The house suddenly became a cage too small to hold her. After flitting about, making feeble starts at one job or another, then moving somewhere else to repeat the aimless action, she told herself she'd just have to get out of the house and let somebody know her good news. Mabel was the first person she thought of but decided she might have bothered her enough already. She had to tell somebody!

She started to the phone but couldn't make up her mind whom to call. She went out on the front porch and looked around. Things certainly looked better out there! What a shame that the side rail had been broken. She remembered seeing Lorena Satterfield cleaning up behind her house. She'd tell her. As she started down the steps, gripping the banister with both hands, she heard the phone ringing.

"Oh, my goodness!" she muttered as she turned around and started back up the steps. "I'm gonna run myself to death today, it looks like." Even as she trudged back inside, she felt yet wouldn't admit how much she was enjoying the inconvenience this endless phone-ringing was causing. "Oh!" she muttered, "maybe it's Mr. Riddick! I bet that's who it is."

It was Virgiline Canfield.

"Etta, I'm so glad I finally got hold of you. I tried several times this mornin' to get you. I got so worried I finally called Marsha Dinwiddie and asked her if she'd heard anything. She said somebody, one of Willie Belle's nephews, I think she said, had been over in your neighborhood and said he thought you were all right. Are you?"

"Yes, Virgiline, I'm fine. It's sweet of you to call. And how are you? Did y'all get any of the tornado?"

"Just some real strong wind, but nothin' major. But what I'm concerned about is you. What about your house?"

She told her and assured her she considered herself fortunate to have come out as well as she did.

"Well, now I'm wonderin', what are you gonna be doin' this evenin'?"

She had to think a while. Her first impulse was to say she was going to be busy, but then she thought better of it. "Well, I don't guess I'm gonna be doin' anything much."

"What about supper? . . . Look, Etta, I'm cookin' a whole batch of food and I wanted to bring it over this evenin'. I thought it might be nice to ask Marsha to eat with us and you could ask Mabel, too. How does that strike you?"

"Why Virgiline, that sounds perfectly wonderful! But I do wish you wouldn't go to a lot of trouble. I do appreciate it, though. It sounds like fun. I'll call Mabel or run over there in a few minutes and ask her. . . . And Virgiline, guess what?"

"What's happened now?"

"I heard from Annette this mornin'. She called and said they're comin' home next week for a while. That is, she and the girls. I'm so excited I can hardly wait. Isn't that wonderful?"

"Oh Etta, it most certainly is. I'm so happy for you, dear. I wanna hear all about it. We'll talk about it tonight, okay?"

"Now wasn't that sweet of Virgiline to ask me to eat with y'all?" Mabel said when Miss Etta mentioned it to her a few minutes later. She playfully slapped Miss Etta's arm and gave a deep, hearty laugh. "I accept! Only Lord knows I ought not to. I just made a pure-dee hog of myself a while ago. It was sort of an eatin' celebration for survivin', you might say."

Miss Etta smiled and reached over and touched Mabel's hand. "It looks like you've been doin' some cleanin' up, too."

Mabel scanned the floor with her eyes. "A little bit. I've spent most of my time tryin' to get hold of that TV man to see if he can come fix my antenna. Somebody I talked to a while ago said he's all tied up with folks over around the shoppin' center and there's no tellin' when I'll be able to get 'im to come fix mine. That disgusts me!" She chuckled. "I think that's why I ate so much a while ago."

Miss Etta laughed. She was in the right mood to appreciate Mabel's sense of humor. She felt so close to her, especially after their talk this morning. "Have you heard from your brother Carl yet?" she asked as she sat down.

Mabel sucked through her teeth, then uttered a mild oath as she bent down to pick up a piece of glass she'd missed. "Yeah, he called a while ago. Didn't seem too concerned, though. That's Carl for you."

"Maybe he tried to call earlier and couldn't get you. Some of the people that called me said they'd had trouble gettin' me."

Mabel pulled down on her skirt but couldn't get it over her pale plump knees. She sucked again and brushed her hand across the arm of the chair. "Maybe. But never mind. Carl's got his own troubles."

She knew what that meant. Carl's sister-in-law Isabel lived with him and Ethel. Carl was Mabel's only living relative and it worried her that Isabel made his life so miserable.

Miss Etta stood and walked over to the broken window. She

leaned forward and looked at the sawed chinaberry tree that Albert had stacked temporarily between her house and Mabel's garage. Her bedroom windows looked awful! She'd have to cover them in the meantime to keep bugs out. She leaned farther forward and tried to see Mabel's car. "What about your car? Was it damaged by the tree?"

Mabel got up, came over, and stood by her. "Just a little. See that place on the trunk? Oh well, thank God it wasn't any worse. I was lookin' at Irene Sanders' car a while ago and it's a mess. It's gonna cost her at least a thousand dollars to have it fixed. Lord yes, I consider myself lucky."

Miss Etta went back to her chair and sat down. She played with the seams of her skirt. She couldn't hold back any longer. "Well, I had a wonderful surprise a while ago."

Mabel sat down with a grunt. "You did? And what was that?"

She smiled to herself, then looked across at Mabel, who had propped her elbow on the arm of the chair and her hand under her chin. "Annette called a while ago."

"You don't mean it!" She clapped her chubby hands together and gave a happy yell. "Bless patty, I've been hopin' and prayin' she would. Go on, Etta, tell me all about it. What'd she say?"

Excitedly and lovingly she related every detail of the conversation. When she mentioned the proposed trip to Germany for Christmas, she said she'd been thinking about it and had decided she'd go.

Mabel hollered again and ran over and hugged her. "Fayetta, that's the best news I've heard in a month of Sundays! I'm so happy I don't know what to do. Lord God! And you say they're comin' next Wednesday?"

She nodded and covered her mouth to keep from laughing outright.

"Then we'd better start thinkin' about where we go'n' put 'em. Now Etta, you know they're welcome to stay here. There ain't no use in you tryin' to fix up a bed for 'em in your livin' room. You know I've got extra bedrooms, so you don't have to worry about where they're gonna sleep. . . . Say, come on in the kitchen and let's have a cup of coffee. And oh, by the way, I've got some home-made peach ice cream I thought I'd bring over tonight. You reckon Virgiline'd mind? . . . Sit down, Etta. How 'bout somethin' to eat? I bet you ain't had no lunch yet, have you?"

She spent the next hour or so calling her students to remind them of the recital rehearsal Thursday evening. She was able to contact most of them. All except Mollie Hong. When Mrs. Hong answered the phone and told her Mollie would be away until later that afternoon, Miss Etta asked that Mollie please return her call at her convenience.

A little before three o'clock, her mind and her body by mutual consent shifted into limited service and she finally admitted to herself that she was exhausted. She picked up yesterday's paper and yawned time and time again as she lay down on her neatly-made, glass-free bed. She put both pillows behind her head and lay for a minute or two, looking around the room and finally to the crippled windows. She still found it hard to believe what had happened. She didn't realize that until she'd had enough sleep to purge her mind she wouldn't be able to see things in proper perspective.

And there was Annette, a lilting rondo tune, recurring consistently, edging in between the more somber tunes and giving a happy unity to what might otherwise be a rueful song. She cheered instantly at the thought. She smiled wearily and closed her eyes just long enough to thank God for the happy way things had turned out.

She felt much better when she awoke later, though slightly disoriented. It took only one look at her paneless windows to put her back in touch. She bathed and dressed up for the coming party. She couldn't remember when she had been so excited and happy. Brother Butler and his wife dropped by for a few minutes as he'd promised, and while the three of them held hands in front of the piano, he said a long, rambling prayer. After they left, Loretta Finley and Fidelia Burnside, two members of her Sunday School class, stopped by and asked her, after a short visit, if she'd like to take a ride around Montcrief to see some of the tornado damage. She told them she had friends coming by later but appreciated the invitation. She was glad she had an honest excuse. The last thing on earth she wanted right now was to see more devastation!

It took all three of them to bring in the food Virgiline had prepared. Some of it had to be reheated, she said, and the Parker House rolls would have to be baked. While that was being done and before Mabel came over, Virgiline and Marsha wanted to see what the bedroom looked like. They both hugged Miss Etta and said how sorry they were, but she didn't cry. She stiffened her back, lifted her chin, and said she considered herself mighty lucky and was thankful it hadn't been worse.

"Yoo-hoo!" It was Mabel.

"Did you lock the front door, Etta?" Virgiline asked.

"No." She started to the living room. "It's open, Mabel."

The others followed. There was a round of hugging, God-praising, and happy chatter.

"What's that you've got in that bag, Mabel?" Virgiline asked.

Mabel held the bag up in front of her. "Some of the best homemade peach ice cream you ever put a tongue to."

"Now Mabel," Virgiline said, "I've done made a cream cheese pound cake for dessert. You didn't need to make ice cream."

Mabel went to the kitchen and put it in the freezer. "Maybe not, but your cream cheese pound cake's gonna taste mighty good with my peach ice cream!"

Marsha and Mabel sat down at the table in the kitchen, and Miss Etta started clearing off the dining room table while Virgiline worked at the stove. She walked to the kitchen door. "Y'all haven't seen my new tablecloth, have you? Come here. I want you to see it."

"Oh, isn't that beautiful!" Marsha said and held up the edge to see the embroidery. "My word, look at all that work! Where'd you get it, Etta?"

The others examined it also.

"Mrs. Barrett gave it to me. . . . You know, Gamaliel's mother. She made it."

"You don't mean it, Etta," Virgiline said and hurried back to the kitchen when she remembered something on the stove. "Hey, I could use some help in here," she added.

Mabel and Marsha took the hint.

As Miss Etta got out the china and silver, she realized how long it had been since she'd used it. She had planned to use it the day she had Mr. Riddick for lunch but decided it might seem pretentious. Some of the pieces needed wiping off. When she went to the kitchen to get a cloth, Marsha put her arm lovingly around her and asked if she needed any help with the table. She said she didn't.

She returned to the dining room to set the table. As she laid things out carefully and precisely and stood back a time or two to check the symmetry of her spacing, she was aware of an excitement and happiness unlike anything she had felt for a long, long time. She reveled in the contrast of her green-rimmed china against the new tablecloth and the way the crystal played in the light like exhilarated children who've been long confined and now allowed to go outside. She listened to Virgiline, Mabel, and Marsha as they talked and laughed in the kitchen, and she knew this moment was special.

It was special, indeed, yet she felt assuredly that she had lived it before. What was it, she wondered. She hadn't dreamed it; it had actually happened. Then, while she was replacing the centerpiece, an ornate candelabra with leaning, dull-hued candles, she remembered. She walked to the window, clasped her hands under her chin, and thought back to that cold February day years ago when Annette celebrated her eleventh birthday. She could hear the children now almost as she had heard them then. She recalled the thrill of hearing "Chopsticks" on a piano that had been muzzled into months of silence.

To be sure, there was some sadness in her reverie. In a way, Annette's birthday party had been the end of one very dreadful phase of her life and the beginning, or at least the anticipation, of a happier time. Annette had been one of the children whose youth and relative permanence were to become the cornerstone of her new fortress. On Wednesday, Annette would come home, back into her life. And maybe, if God would help her, she would make a special effort to see that she didn't lose her again.

She walked back to the table and smiled at the hope and promise it represented of a new beginning. She laughed silently to herself as she listened again to her friends in the kitchen. Before rejoining them, she closed her eyes and repeated a part of her favorite psalm, "'Thou hast put gladness in my heart more than in the time that their corn and their wine increased.'"

Just as they sat down to eat, the phone rang. She muttered a few words of displeasure as she got up to answer it.

"Etta, for God's sake," Mabel shouted after her, "tell 'em we're eatin' supper."

Suddenly she remembered! It must be Mr. Riddick! He'd probably had to come back to Montcrief. She almost dropped the phone in her excitement.

It was Mollie Hong.

"Hello, Miss Etta. I'm sorry I missed your call. How are you? I've been worried about you."

It took a few moments to adjust her thinking. "Why, I'm fine, Mollie. Just fine! I asked your mother to have you call me because there was somethin' special I wanted to ask you."

"Mother told me about the rehearsal. But I already knew that."

"Yes, I know, dear. But I wanted to ask you for a very special favor. Will you do it for Miss Etta?"

Mollie laughed. "Of course I will, Miss Etta, if I possibly can."

She hesitated. In those few moments of waiting, she remembered so many spring recitals and so many Aprils when she was a young girl and woman. She took a deep breath and gave a soft, happy laugh. "I was wonderin', Mollie dear, if you would let Miss Etta have some more of those beautiful sweet peas to put on the stage for our recital."

For Reference

Not to be taken from this room